Elizabeth Ferrars and The Murder Room

›› This title is part of The Murder Room, our series dedicated to making available out-of-print or hard-to-find titles by classic crime writers.

Crime fiction has always held up a mirror to society. The Victorians were fascinated by sensational murder and the emerging science of detection; now we are obsessed with the forensic detail of violent death. And no other genre has so captivated and enthralled readers.

Vast troves of classic crime writing have for a long time been unavailable to all but the most dedicated frequenters of second-hand bookshops. The advent of digital publishing means that we are now able to bring you the backlists of a huge range of titles by classic and contemporary crime writers, some of which have been out of print for decades.

From the genteel amateur private eyes of the Golden Age and the femmes fatales of pulp fiction, to the morally ambiguous hard-boiled detectives of mid twentieth-century America and their descendants who walk our twenty-first century streets, The Murder Room has it all. ››

The Murder Room
Where Criminal Minds Meet

themurderroom.com

Elizabeth Ferrars (1907–1995)

One of the most distinguished crime writers of her generation, Elizabeth Ferrars was born Morna Doris MacTaggart in Rangoon and came to Britain at the age of six. She was a pupil at Bedales school between 1918 and 1924, studied journalism at London University and published her first crime novel, *Give a Corpse a Bad Name*, in 1940, the year that she met her second husband, academic Robert Brown. Highly praised by critics, her brand of intelligent, gripping mysteries was also beloved by readers. She wrote over seventy novels and was also published (as E. X. Ferrars) in the States, where she was equally popular. *Ellery Queen Mystery Magazine* described her as 'the writer who may be the closest of all to Christie in style, plotting and general milieu', and the *Washington Post* called her 'a consummate professional in clever plotting, characterization and atmosphere'. She was a founding member of the Crime Writers Association, who, in the early 1980s, gave her a lifetime achievement award.

By Elizabeth Ferrars
(published in The Murder Room)

Skeleton Staff

Elizabeth Ferrars

An Orion book

Copyright © Peter MacTaggart 1969

The right of Elizabeth Ferrars to be identified as the author of this work has been asserted in accordance with the Copyright, Designs and Patents Act 1988.

This edition published by
The Orion Publishing Group Ltd
Orion House
5 Upper St Martin's Lane
London WC2H 9EA

An Hachette UK company
A CIP catalogue record for this book is available from the British Library

ISBN 978 1 4719 0666 4

www.orionbooks.co.uk

This story takes place on the island of Madeira, but all the characters in it are imaginary, and if any of them has been called by the name of a real person, it was entirely accidental.

CHAPTER I

"I DON'T believe it."

A pause.

"I *don't* believe it."

Roberta Ellison was talking to herself, as she had been doing increasingly lately.

Luckily she seemed not to mind being overheard. In fact, thought Camilla Carey, her younger sister, as she lay half-asleep on a white wicker chair on the small, palm-shaded terrace, sometimes it was almost as if Roberta intended to be overheard. She did not lower her voice and she said things which it often turned out later she had wanted Camilla to know.

Why she did not simply say them to Camilla's face in the first place was an interesting problem. The old Roberta would certainly have done so. She had always felt entitled to say to Camilla's face anything she chose. About Camilla's face, sometimes. About her clothes, her abilities, her morals, her friends. Tact, Roberta had taken for granted, was not required of an elder sister. So there was something very intriguing about this new devious way that she had developed of letting Camilla know what was in her mind.

"She seems such a nice girl," Roberta went on in a thoughtful but carrying voice. "A charming girl. I liked her. Yes, I did. I really liked her."

Another pause.

"No," Roberta said. "I shan't say anything about it. No one would believe me."

She was in the sitting-room and Camilla's chair was just outside the open french window. It was impossible that Roberta should not have seen her. So it was as if Roberta were giving advance warning that in a moment she would be coming out on to the terrace to discuss some problem concerning Julie Davy. Because it was of Julie, obviously,

1

that she was talking. A pity, because a morning of swimming and sunbathing, followed by a substantial lunch, had left Camilla feeling very agreeably drowsy and quite incapable of dealing with anyone's problems.

But sooner Roberta's than her own. Those really would not bear thinking about.

Opening her eyes briefly, blinking at the sun-washed hillside, at the green of the banana plantation below the garden and the red pantile roofs of the other small cream-coloured houses like this one that covered the slope down to the sea, Camilla closed her eyes again and waited.

A moment later she heard the soft tapping of Roberta's rubber-tipped crutches on the terrace and her dragging footsteps.

"Camilla, are you awake?" she asked. "Camilla, I want you to tell me something. Do you believe in first impressions?"

Camilla blinked her eyes open again and groped about on the ground beside her chair.

"Can you see my glasses?" she asked.

"They're under your chair," said Roberta.

Camilla reached under the chair, found the glasses, put them on and looked up at her sister.

Actually they were half-sisters. They had had the same father, a country solicitor, but different mothers. There were seventeen years between them and not many resemblances. Roberta was fair, Camilla was dark. Roberta was a beauty, Camilla was not, though there was a certain awkward elegance about her abrupt gestures and something arresting in her narrow, sharp-featured face. Roberta had married early and happily. Camilla was twenty-eight and not married at all.

But as always now, when Camilla saw Roberta, even when it was after an interval of only an hour or so, she felt the shock of a distressing pity. Camilla had never fully recognised before what the loss of one human being can do to another. Since the day, a month ago, when her brother-in-law, Justin Ellison, had suddenly collapsed with a cerebral haemorrhage in one of the main streets of Funchal and died a few hours later, Roberta's face had aged by ten years. It had aged and changed far more than it had after the car accident, four years ago, from which she had emerged a cripple, unable to walk without crutches.

It had been after the accident that she and Justin had come to live on Madeira. Before that Justin had been a surgeon in a London hospital, a successful man, only thirty-nine, which was two years younger than Roberta. A witty, quiet, vigorous, wonderfully warm-hearted man. He should have had a long career ahead of him. But he had given it up to bring Roberta to a place where there would always be sunshine, colour, warmth to soothe pain and that other very important thing, the certainty of being able to obtain domestic help. And the treatment, up to a point, had been successful. Roberta had lost neither the rounded, young-looking attractiveness of her face, nor a certain cheerful courage which had enabled her to enjoy life.

But beauty and cheerfulness and courage had all gone now. Her skin looked withered, her blue eyes stared, her light golden hair was lifeless. She looked uncertain, bewildered and lost. And for the first time in her life she needed Camilla. Which happened, just then, to be very unfortunate for Camilla.

"You haven't answered," Roberta said as she lowered herself cautiously into a chair facing Camilla and leant her metal crutches against a table beside her. "Do you?"

"Do I what?" Camilla asked.

"Believe in first impressions? Do you believe first impressions mean anything?"

"I believe they mean something, but what they generally tell you is something about yourself and not necessarily true about the thing that's making the impression."

"Then you don't believe in them."

"I've just said I do."

Camilla's spectacles had some grit sticking to them that they had picked up from the ground where she had put them down when she dozed off after lunch. She took them

3

off and polished them on the hem of the blue cotton shirt that she was wearing with a pair of scarlet jeans.

"Oh, you always twist things so," Roberta said. "You always try to be subtle. Now I do believe in first impressions. I always have. And I've found again and again that it's when I don't trust them or ignore them that I get into trouble."

Camilla put her glasses on again and her slightly fuzzy vision of her sister came into focus. Roberta, wearing one of her expensive, simple dresses which was of striped grey and white silk, was watching her with her new staring intensity. But as soon as Camilla's eyes met hers, Roberta dropped them to the cigarette that she was lighting.

Camilla said, "You're telling me you'd a bad first impression of Julie Davy."

"No. . . . Well. . . . But I mean just that very first momentary thing you get when you first see a person. It's gone almost before you know it's happened." Roberta's gaze followed the trail of the smoke that drifted from her lips on to the still air. "Then you start seeing details about them, eyes, nose, mouth, the way they're dressed, the way they look at you. I remember thinking at that stage that everything was going to turn out wonderfully. I like having good-looking people about and Julie's perfect to look at. And she's so kind and she's been so quick at learning how to help me and when not to. That's important, you know—not always to be fussing round, making me feel helpless. If she'd been a fusser and pillow-plumper-up I quite simply shouldn't have been able to stand her."

Reluctantly Camilla pulled herself upright in the long, lounging chair, and slid her slim, scarlet-clad legs to the ground. Any trouble to do with Julie Davy, who had come out from England a week ago to be Roberta's nurse and companion so that Camilla could go home, was serious, was a crisis. It could not be ignored. It was necessary for Camilla to wake up properly and try to be forceful and practical.

But being forceful and practical did not come naturally

to her, except sometimes when it concerned only herself. Where others were concerned, she was inclined to dodge responsibility.

"Exactly what's the matter with Julie, apart from this first impression thing?" she asked.

"Which you don't think is important."

"If you've decided you don't like her, that's important."

"But I do like her and I've been thinking these last few days how incredibly lucky we were to have found her," Roberta said. "It was just that when she first came, when you fetched her from the airport and she walked in, I had this—sort of recoil. A sort of immediate and intense distrust. If you don't know what I'm talking about, you don't."

"I think I do, only I didn't feel it with Julie."

It was safe for them to discuss the girl because she had the afternoons off and to-day had taken the car to the Tourist Club for a swim there. It did not matter if Ione, the Portuguese maid, a good-natured little dumpling of a woman, overheard them, since she spoke hardly any English.

"Well, perhaps I didn't really feel anything either," Roberta said. "I suppose I'm rather distrustful of all strangers nowadays because I'm so helpless. I never used to be like that. It isn't my real nature. I like people. I take to them easily. Too easily, I expect, because I so want them to like me. That was how I started feeling about Julie after that first queer shudder I had. I became terribly anxious that she should take to me and want to stay here—though God knows why she should, a young thing like that, apart, of course, from the chance of having a free holiday on Madeira. Only looking after me won't be exactly a holiday, will it? And I know I'm not the brightest of company. When you've gone and there's no one here even near her own age she'll find things dull as hell. So she'll go too. Have you thought about that, Camilla? I've been wondering, perhaps we ought to have looked for someone older."

"Roberta," Camilla said, "I suppose you really won't consider coming home to England."

5

Roberta picked up one of her crutches and jabbed gently with its rubber tip at a small lizard near her feet. The lizard was too quick for her, as they always were, and vanished with a flick of its tail between two stones.

"You know all the arguments against it," she said. "This is my home, I've got friends here, the climate suits me, and I haven't got that ghastly anxiety I'd have in England about whether or not I could get a maid. After all, here at a pinch I can manage without you or Julie or anyone. But where would I be without Ione?" Her voice suddenly went up a tone into a sort of muted shrillness. "I'm not just trying to be difficult, Camilla, really I'm not. I know I've been a burden this last month, but I honestly think I'll manage to be more independent of you and altogether less trouble if I stay here than I ever should in England."

Whenever that note came into Roberta's voice, Camilla cringed inwardly because of her own health and strength. Generally she made some almost violent movement to get rid of the sensation. Now, standing up, she started to walk up and down the terrace.

It was built up about six feet above the garden, with steps at one end leading down. The garden was built up in the same way above the banana plantation. The whole steep hillside was terraced, like much of this mountainous island.

"About Julie, then," Camilla said. "What's happened to turn you against her?"

Roberta's hand shot out. She had been waiting for this moment. She held a piece of paper. "Look—only I wasn't going to tell you anything about it, because I know you won't believe me."

Camilla looked at the paper, which appeared to be a bill, but, being in Portuguese, meant nothing to her.

"I don't understand it," she said.

"It's my monthly bill from Godhino's." Godhino was the chemist from whom Roberta bought most of her drugs and cosmetics. "And all those items at the bottom—they're suntan lotion and cleansing-cream and toilet water and two lipsticks—I didn't order any of them."

"Then Godhino's have made a mistake. They've put something on your bill that should have gone on somebody else's."

"But the things are all in Julie's room."

"How do you know?"

"I went to see."

Jolted, Camilla stood still. The house was Roberta's; she had the right, Camilla supposed, to go into any part of it. That still didn't make it a pleasant thought that she went uninvited into Julie's room when Julie was not there.

"I still think there's been some mistake," Camilla said. "You can probably sort it out on the telephone. If you can't, I'll drive you down to talk to them or go and see them myself and see what I can do with my phrase-book."

"The things are in a drawer of Julie's dressing-table," Roberta said.

"Oh, you look through her drawers too."

Roberta suddenly hammered hard on the ground with one of her crutches.

"Can't you understand, Camilla? Won't you even try? I'm not like you. I'm dependent on other people. I have to know what sort of people they are. I can't afford to take chances. You'll be going away soon and I'll be in this girl's clutches. If you don't believe what I'm telling you about her, go and look for yourself. The things are in the top right-hand drawer of the dressing-table. You may not like the idea of looking, but it's better for you to do that than think I've suddenly developed persecution mania and taken to making crazy attacks on innocent people."

"Oh, I believe the things are there," Camilla said. "I'm sure they are. You wouldn't make that up."

"Well then?"

Camilla sat down again on the edge of the white wicker chair, took her glasses off and gave them another unnecessary polish.

Without them the little garden turned into a pleasing abstract in which it was tempting to let her thoughts wander. The tall royal palm was only a brownish streak topped by a

7

tuft of grey-green fronds and some creamy, silken tassels. The bouganvillæa clothing the wrought-iron fence that enclosed the garden was a smudge of blazing purple. A frangipani, covered in blossom, was a mysterious intricacy of lines, speckled with dabs of peach-colour.

"It's the way you jump to conclusions," Camilla said after a little. "Suppose Julie did order the things at Godhino's and have them put on your account. Wasn't that the easiest thing for her to do, since she can't talk Portuguese? She could simply point at what she wanted and give your name and address."

"Then tell me she'd done it and pay me back?"

"Of course."

"I hadn't thought of that," Roberta admitted. "But then why hasn't she said anything about it yet?"

"She may have forgotten, but she'll probably do it when she thinks of it."

"Oh, I suppose you're right." Roberta spoke fretfully and plainly did not mean what she said. "You so often are, except about yourself. Your own life's a mess, isn't it? But really it's terribly difficult for me now, having to rely on strangers. I wish you understood."

"I do," Camilla said.

"Justin used to cope with everything, you see."

"I know."

"I expect he sheltered me too much. Since we knew I was going to be like this always, I expect it would have been better if he'd made me a bit more self-reliant. But we never thought, we never dreamt of the possibility that he could go first. He was younger than me, and never ill. . . ."

"I know, I know."

"So you wouldn't mind too much if I asked you to cope with this for me now, would you?"

Camilla sat up straighter. She put on her spectacles and took a hard look into her sister's face. It had the kind of smile on it which in the days of her beauty had made people ready to do anything for her and she was still sure of its power, which really was rather pathetic and embarrassing.

"You mean, just get rid of her for you, don't you?" Camilla said.

"Oh, deal somehow with the whole horrid business. Ask her if she did order the things. Put it nicely, of course. Say she needn't bother to pay me back, if you like. I don't mind giving her the things, though I must say she's got expensive tastes. All the same, I really don't mind, if only she's frank with me about it. It's the feeling of something underhand going on that I can't stand. And you going away soon, leaving me with someone who'd do a thing like that. Just think of what she might do next, if we let her get away with it."

"All right." Camilla knew that she would not be able to avoid the disagreeable job of questioning Julie Davy; and because she was the kind of basically irresolute person who has to do a thing at once or may not be able to bring herself to do it at all, she added, "I'll speak to her as soon as she gets in. Only I wonder . . . I wonder if it wouldn't be best to discuss it with Matthew first."

This suddenly seemed a wonderful idea to her. Matthew Frensham was an old friend of Justin's and Roberta's and lived only a few doors away. He had helped Roberta in all kinds of ways since Justin's death and Camilla found him a sympathetic, steadying person. "After all, he's an ex-policeman, it's right up his street," she said.

But Roberta shook her head irritably. "I can't be eternally bothering him. I've asked too much of him already. And the issues are quite simple. If Julie says she didn't order the things, we'll know she's lying, because after all they're *there*. If she admits she did order them and says she meant to pay me for them, then we'll say no more about it."

"And what will you do if she leaves here?" Camilla asked.

There was a pause, then Roberta answered, "I'll have to look for somebody else."

"And meanwhile?"

"I'll manage as best I can with Ione."

"If you think I'm going to stay on indefinitely . . ."

"I don't. I know you can't."

"Just so long as that's understood."

"My dear Camilla, I know you've got to go home. I know you've got your work."

Roberta always managed to make Camilla's work sound like an eccentricity, instead of something that she had to do for a living. She was a textile designer, did a certain amount of interior decoration and some advertising work when she could get it, and if she was not brilliant, she worked hard and took what she did very seriously.

"And I know you've got other problems," Roberta went on. "That's partly why I want to get this wretched business with Julie settled quickly—so that we'll know where we are and you *can* go home. Though why you're so anxious to and how you can even think of taking up again with a man who treated you as he did is quite beyond me. I personally shouldn't dream of marrying anyone like that. But that's your affair."

"There isn't much chance of my marrying him, I've told you that," Camilla said.

"Then of becoming his mistress—or are you that already?" A curious gleam came into Roberta's eyes. "Is that part of the problem? I often wonder about you, you know—how you really live all by yourself in London. But it's all right, I know you'll never tell me. You never really tell me anything about yourself. We aren't at all alike. I'm a frank sort of person. It just feels natural to me to tell people everything about myself. But you're terribly secretive. It rather scares me sometimes."

Camilla's face had turned expressionless. She knew that it was true that she was secretive, but it was Roberta, years before, with her habit of trampling casually on Camilla's highly sensitive, immature feelings, who had taught her to be. Had taught her that what a person didn't know, she couldn't kill.

Standing up, Camilla said, "There's Julie now."

She had just heard the sound of the car, which she recognised as Roberta's, labouring up the hill.

10

"Oh, be nice to her!" Roberta exclaimed as Camilla turned towards the door. "Be tactful. Don't say anything you can possibly help to upset her."

Remarkable instructions, Camilla thought, as she went into the house. Be nice to her, be tactful, don't upset her—just tell her she's a cheat and a thief and sack her, please. . . .

She met Julie Davy in the little dim hall of the house, which was all on one floor, so that Roberta never had to struggle up and down stairs, unless she wanted to go down from the terrace into the garden.

Julie came in with a light, swinging stride, wearing a sleeveless beach dress of white towelling, gold sandals, sunglasses and an enormous straw hat. The new tan on her long, slim arms and legs glistened with sun-tan oil. Her chestnut hair hung in a wet mass down her back, its wetness making it spring into a great cluster of curls.

Seeing Camilla, she took off her sunglasses and her hat.

"How d'you like my lovely hat?" she asked gaily and spun it on a finger. "Isn't it lovely? They have the loveliest hats here and they cost nothing—just *nothing*. I saw it in that place at the bottom of the hill, and I went in, feeling awfully brave, ready to speak my three words of Portuguese, but of course they spoke wonderful English."

She had a pointed, rather elfin face, big, grey, gentle eyes and a slender body, all flowing, flexible curves. She seemed artless and not very clever and cheerful and kind.

Camilla had found her for Roberta by putting advertisements in some Sunday papers. Replying, Julie had written that she was twenty-three, had just acquired a domestic science diploma, had no actual nursing qualifications, but had helped to look after an arthritic grandmother, and had given the head of her college and a bishop, who was her uncle, as references. When she had arrived in Funchal she had seemed to Camilla the perfect answer to the problem of Roberta.

Had she been too perfect?

Looking at Julie now as she stood there laughing, twirling

11

her hat on her finger, Camilla found it very difficult to doubt her honest and happy good-nature. But she did not really doubt Roberta either. Roberta was not given to saying things that could easily be shown to be untrue.

Feeling a fearful urge to get a detestable job done quickly, Camilla stopped Julie as she was going to her room and said, "Just a minute, Julie—can I speak to you?"

Julie waited, smiling. There was no uneasiness in the smile. It was that of a person who assumes that only something pleasant can be about to happen.

Camilla hurried on, "There seems to have been a mistake of some sort that I want to get straightened out. It's about some things that were ordered from Godhino's in Funchal. Did you order anything there?"

"Godhino's?" The name seemed to convey nothing to Julie.

"A chemist," Camilla said. "They seem to have charged my sister for a number of things she didn't order. She wondered if they were really for you."

Julie shook her head slowly from side to side. Drops from her wet hair fell on the waxed floor of the hall.

"The only shop I've been in is the one where I got this hat. They've such *lots* of lovely hats there! I'd have liked to buy half a dozen."

"The things were some cleansing-cream and sun-tan lotion and things like that."

"Oh . . . !" It came out as a smothered gasp. The happiness went out of Julie's bright eyes like a light put out. A wave of pink swept over her face. "How stupid of me," she murmured in a low voice. "A mistake. I didn't think of that."

"What *did* you think?" Camilla was dismayed at such a marked reaction to her questioning. She had really been hoping that somehow it would turn out that Julie knew nothing about the goods from Godhino's.

"I thought . . . They were there, you see, in my room. In one of my drawers actually." Julie's cheeks were even redder now and the words came tumbling out in a jumbled hurry of embarrassment. "I thought they were meant to be a surprise. A present. I was so glad because I thought it meant . . . Well, that Mrs. Ellison was pleased with me. I'm afraid I used one of the lipsticks straight away. But if it was just a mistake I can pay for that and the other things can be sent back. I'm so sorry. I—it was very stupid."

"It sounds very natural." Camilla, intensely embarrassed too, did not know what to do next.

"Could I see the things?" she asked. "Would you mind showing them to me?"

"Of course not. But I'm sorry I was so silly. It must have been worrying for you wondering what had happened. Come along." Julie darted into her room.

It was a small room, next to Roberta's, with a window that faced towards the road. A vine on the wall outside half-covered the window and the light in the room was coolly green. There was a bed with a flowered cretonne cover, a painted chest of drawers with a mirror fixed to the wall above it, a chair, a built-in dress cupboard. On the chest of drawers was a small terra-cotta jar with a few pale blue sprays of plumbago in it, and also a photograph of two pleasant-looking, middle-aged people, a man and a woman, obviously Julie's parents. The room was tidy except for the clothes that Julie had been wearing before she went for her swim, which had been thrown down on the bed.

She went swiftly across the room, opened the top right-hand drawer of the chest of drawers and stood aside for Camilla to look inside it.

They were all there, the things that Roberta had mentioned, along with some nylons, handkerchiefs, hair-rollers and other odds and ends.

"Yes. Well." Camilla stood there, feeling helpless. After a moment she pushed the drawer shut. "Perhaps they were a present," she muttered. "Perhaps I'm the one who's made a muddle of things."

"No, they weren't, you're only saying that to make me not feel a fool," Julie answered. "I'm awfully sorry I was so stupid."

"When did you find them there?" Camilla asked.

"Just before I went to swim."

"Actually in your drawer?"

"Yes."

"Then why didn't you say anything about it?"

"Because I . . . Well, I . . . I was puzzled. I *thought* they were a present, and I wanted to come out and say thank you, but Mrs. Ellison had gone to lie down in her room and I didn't want to disturb her, and you looked as if you were asleep on the terrace, and in a way it seemed rather odd, just finding them there like that, so I thought I'd wait till I got back and ask you. How *did* they get into my drawer if they weren't meant for me?"

"Someone made a mistake," Camilla said. "A bad mistake, I'm afraid. I think much the best thing now would be to forget it. And do please take them as a present from me. Won't you, please?"

"Oh no, I couldn't do that." Julie reddened again. "I mean, if they weren't really meant for me and you're just being kind because I've been so stupid . . . Oh!" She gave another startled gasp. The pupils of her eyes dilated. "Oh, I believe I'm beginning to understand! Oh, I really *am* stupid. I've just realised, you think I ordered these things from whatever-his-name-is, and hoped Mrs. Ellison would pay for them without noticing!"

"No," Camilla said. "No, really——"

"Yes, you do." Julie sat down abruptly on the bed, staring at Camilla in horror. "But why? What is there about me to make you think a thing like that?"

"For God's sake don't cry!" Camilla said as she saw Julie's eyes fill with tears. "I told you, the best thing is to forget this happened. If you don't want the things as a present from me, I'll keep them myself."

Julie dabbed at her eyes with a corner of the damp towel that she had brought back from the shore with her.

"No. I'm still being stupid," she said. "You don't really think I ordered these things. You put them here yourself."

"I did *what*?"

"You or Mrs. Ellison. Put them here to have a reason for getting rid of me. It's very like last time."

"What last time?" Camilla asked.

"Oh, in my first job. It was in a horrible little private school. I went there as assistant matron and they found something wrong with my accounts and they said I must have done it on purpose. But I didn't. I know there was something wrong with the accounts, but it wasn't on purpose. It was just that I'm not much good at arithmetic. At least, that's what I thought at the time, but later I actually started wondering if someone else hadn't done it on purpose. The matron was always horrid to me. I believe she was afraid I was after her job. And then she started getting jealous as well, because I went out a few times with one of the masters and nobody ever took her out. I'm sure now, almost sure, it was her doing, the muddle in the accounts and me being sacked. But you needn't have done this to me, you know. You could just have told me I wasn't what you wanted. I'd have been very sorry, but it wouldn't have felt as awful as this."

"I thought this was your first job," Camilla said. "Your references made it sound as if you were coming here straight from that domestic science college."

"I'm sure they didn't actually say so," Julie answered. "I'm sure neither my uncle nor Miss Wainwright would tell a downright lie. But they both thought I'd had a rotten deal at the school and that the best thing would be to say nothing about it and act as if this was my first job."

"And your uncle a bishop!" Camilla gave a wry smile. "How many jobs have you actually had?"

"Just that one at the school."

Julie began to rub her hair absent-mindedly with the damp towel. "But what I don't understand is why this sort of thing happens to me. What is it about me? At the

15

school I'm fairly sure it was one person's jealousy, but here . . . Who is there to be jealous of me about what? . . . Oh!" Again she gave the exclamation with which she signalled the entry of a new idea into her head. Behind the haze of tears her gaze sharpened. "Are you afraid Mrs. Ellison's showing signs of liking me too much? Suppose I use undue influence, or whatever it's called, when you go. She's quite rich, isn't she? And an invalid. And lonely. Yes, I suppose it's quite possible you might be afraid of me."

There was no anger in Julie's tone, only a sort of wonderment, and she nodded her head thoughtfully, as if she had found a plain solution to her problem. Then suddenly she sprang to her feet, wrenched open the drawer where the cosmetics were, grabbed them with both hands and held them out.

"Take them, take them!" she cried. "I used the lipstick, I'll keep it, I'll pay for it. But take the rest!"

Camilla did not argue. She let Julie thrust the jars and bottles into her hands, then went out, expecting to hear the door slammed behind her.

After a moment it was, though not very violently.

On the terrace Roberta was sitting where Camilla had left her. Camilla could see her there from the hall, with something expectant, almost eager, in her attitude.

It was that eagerness that suddenly made Camilla feel that she could not stand another talk with her, and so, as she was starting across the sitting-room, she stopped abruptly, put down what she was carrying on a table and turned back to the hall.

She heard Roberta call her but took no notice, opening the front door, stepping out on to the short path which led under a vine-covered trellis to the road and starting to walk up it.

CHAPTER II

WITHOUT A HAT or the dark eye-shades that clipped on to her glasses, the afternoon sunshine felt overpowering and she could feel the heat of the rough cobbles of the road through the soles of her sandals. But she had not far to go. Passing the next-door house, she turned in at the gate of the one beyond it and went up the short path between two hibiscus bushes which were covered all over in rosy bloom, to the green-painted door. The house was very like Roberta's, cream-washed, with a roof of red pantiles and built out on one floor above a small terraced garden. Camilla knocked on the door, waited a moment, knocked again, and when there was still no answer, took the path round the house to the back of it.

Before she had turned the corner of it on to the terrace, she heard the clatter of a typewriter. Stop, go, stop, fast, slow, stop. It rattled on jerkily in response to the uneven flow of Matthew Frensham's thoughts. The sound had stopped and he was sitting still for a long moment, a frown on his face as he stared at the sheet of paper in the machine, before he became aware of Camilla, standing before him.

"You're working," she said. "I'm sorry."

He scrambled to his feet. "Yes, I'm working like the devil and I'm so delighted to be interrupted. You've arrived at just the right time for a drink."

It was always the right time for a drink with Matthew and the right time to be interrupted, which had been lucky, during the last month, for Camilla, who had made a habit of dropping in to see him when she was suffering from an overdose of Roberta.

He was a tall, lean man of about fifty, still muscular, with a look about him of having taken a good deal of battering from life and not having been too badly put out by it. He had rough grey hair, sun-browned skin taut over the bone behind and bright dark eyes, set far apart above a rather flattened nose. They were watchful eyes that looked as if they did not miss much. He had been a policeman in East Africa before retiring and coming to Madeira.

"Whisky?" he asked. "Gin? Madeira? Beer?"

"Beer, I think, please."

Brushing a few ants off the seat of a white wicker chair, almost exactly like the one on Roberta's terrace, Camilla sat down, while Matthew disappeared into the house to fetch the drinks, reappearing in a moment with two tall glasses of the cool, pale, fizzy liquid that the Portuguese call beer.

As she took one of them, Camilla asked, "If you don't like writing, Matthew, why do you go on with it?"

It was the story of his life that he was writing. He had been writing it off and on for about three years, and probably, Camilla thought, would still be writing it ten years hence. Writing it was the sort of project that really wasn't meant to be concluded. It was simply something that had helped to keep him going after his wife Moira had been killed up in the mountains above Funchal. She had been driving by herself on the narrow, winding road, cobbled all the way, that went up to high and lonely Eira do Serrado, had run into cloud and driven off the edge of the road, straight into a chasm. The book had been begun a few weeks later. And now, whenever Matthew started working at it, it meant that he was going through a bad patch, that he was in more need than usual of help to fill the emptiness of life. And when he pounded the typewriter, brooded over it, trying to evoke a past that had not been empty, but colourful and adventurous and full of interest, and when he crumpled up page after page of incredibly flat prose, the effort of it all apparently did help a certain amount. Otherwise even he, a dogged, defiant man who hated to be beaten, surely would have abandoned it.

It was to be expected that he should be going through one of his bad patches now, for he and Justin Ellison had been close friends. They had all been friends, Justin, Matthew, Moira and Roberta. It had been largely due to the fact that the Frenshams had already been living on Madeira when Roberta had her accident that the Ellisons had settled there too. The friendship had begun in the schooldays of Moira and Roberta, then the two husbands, when they met, had liked one another and the four of them had somehow become a unit, almost like a family, only closer than families usually are.

Of course, long intervals had passed, years sometimes, when the two couples had seen hardly anything of one another. During the Frenshams' years in East Africa there had been only brief and occasional meetings when the Frenshams were home on leave, or when once or twice the Ellisons had visited them in some outpost of the empire. But a friendship of astonishing strength had survived, and in the end had brought them all to Funchal.

"How is she?" Matthew asked, sitting down again at the table, behind the typewriter.

"Roberta?" Camilla sipped her beer. "I don't know. I wish I did. Matthew, that's what I came to talk about. She's up to something."

"She generally is." He smiled.

"Then again," Camilla said, "perhaps she isn't. Shall I tell you about it?"

"Why not, if it's why you came?"

"I just wish I'd come sooner. You might have stopped me doing something awfully stupid."

"Probably not, but go on."

"Well, it began this afternoon when I heard Roberta talking to herself," she said. "She does a good deal of that now. At first I thought it was simply loneliness, a way of talking to Justin. Then I began to think she was really talking to me, telling me things in that way so that I couldn't argue with her about them. For all I know, she did it to Justin too. To-day she was muttering to herself about how much she'd liked Julie Davy when she first arrived."

"Of course," Matthew said. "She's a charmer."

"Yes, I know, that's how I feel myself. But I'll tell you things in the order they happened. A moment after Roberta had been saying to herself how much she'd liked Julie, she came out to me with a paper in her hand which was a bill from Godhino's in Funchal, which she said had a whole lot of items on it that she hadn't ordered, some pretty expensive cosmetics and sun-tan lotion and so on. And she said she'd just found these things in a drawer in Julie's room. Julie was out having a swim at the time."

"So Roberta's a snoop," he said.

"I'm afraid so."

"Well, don't look as if you expect me to be awfully shocked, my dear," he said. "You don't think Moira and I knew Roberta all those years without being able to take her as she was. Besides, I've done a good deal of snooping too in my time. Policemen do."

"Well then," Camilla went on, "Roberta started saying she couldn't have anyone around whom she couldn't trust completely, and would I please cope with the matter— challenge Julie about having ordered the things, that is, and sack her."

"Ah yes, as Justin would have had to do for her in the past."

"Yes. So I stopped Julie as she was coming in from her swim and asked her what she knew about the things, and she admitted straight away that they were in her room, but said she'd thought they were a present. Then she caught on to what I was more or less accusing her of and began to cry, and asked what there was about her that made this sort of thing happen to her, and let out that she'd been sacked from her last job for supposedly cooking her accounts. While she was at it, of course, she let out that this wasn't her first job, as her references implied, though she said she was sure they hadn't actually stated it. She'd had a job as assistant matron in a school. And then suddenly she turned on me and accused me of having planted the things in her drawer myself so that Roberta would get rid of her. She said Roberta was rich and an invalid and that I was probably afraid Roberta would get too fond of her and perhaps cut me out of her will."

"Well, well. Scheming Camilla. What happened then?"

"I came here."

"Which was a good idea, I was wanting company. But I'm not sure what I can do for you. Do you need me to tell you what you think yourself, that Roberta planted those things in Julie's drawer?"

"Well, did she do that?" Camilla asked.

"I should think, almost certainly."

"What makes you so sure?"

"Just knowing Roberta pretty intimately." He stretched out a hand for Camilla's glass. "Drink that up and I'll get you another."

"No thanks."

"Wait a minute then while I get myself one."

He tilted up his glass, emptied it and disappeared again into the sitting-room.

Returning, he went on, "Roberta's motive's obvious. She wants to keep you here at any price, so she wants you thoroughly convinced there's a good reason for getting rid of Julie, that it isn't just a capricious dislike. Perhaps she doesn't even dislike the girl. But she really can't bear the thought of you going away and leaving her. I don't know if you've realised that. She can't bear the feeling of being left in the care of a stranger. She wants you here to depend on as she depended on Justin. And in a way I don't blame her—no, don't look at me so angrily—I'm only telling you the obvious."

"But I *can't* stay, Matthew! Even if I wanted to, I can't. I've got problems of my own—a decision I've got to take. Every day it's put off it gets harder. I've got to go home."

"Yes, I know how it is. And it probably wouldn't work out if you did stay. Not for long. You're sorry for Roberta and trying to do what you ought for her, but there are limits. You aren't actually very fond of her, are you?"

Camilla lifted a hand a little way, then let it fall back on to her lap.

"It shows as badly as that, does it?"

"Well, it does show."

"I'm sorry. I'm afraid it goes a long way back. When my mother left my father and Roberta had to be a kind of stepmother to me, she wasn't too keen on the job. My childhood wasn't much fun."

"And one never forgives that, does one? Poor Roberta, having to reap what she sowed." But his voice did not sound as if he were really particularly sorry for her, and Camilla suddenly found herself wondering what the limits of his affection for Roberta were. After Moira's death he had seemed to draw even closer to the Ellisons than before, spending so much of his time with them that Camilla knew Roberta had decided that in a quiet and unpassionate fashion he was half in love with her, a belief from which she had derived a good deal of pleasure. And since Justin's death Matthew had been very helpful to her, arranging the funeral, dealing with lawyers, and offering her, when she needed it, a shoulder to cry on. But it was obvious that he had few illusions about her.

"All the same," he resumed, "if you could stay a little . . . I'm not trying to influence you, but if you could stay until Roberta's got someone else to take care of her . . . I'll always do what I can, of course, but it's a woman she needs. And it seems Julie Davy's got to go. Apart from Roberta's distrust of her, it's already in Julie's mind, it seems to me, that Roberta's rich and an invalid and that it might be possible, if she plays her cards well, to be left something in Roberta's will."

"Oh no, I don't think that for a moment," Camilla said. "I never meant to give you that impression of her."

"But you said she accused you of being afraid she might try to do just that, which shows it's in her mind. A good many accusations tell you more about the person who makes them than the person they're made about. I'm beginning to think perhaps I don't like your Julie as much as I thought I did."

"I think she may simply have thought she'd found a reasonable explanation of what had happened," Camilla said. "It *is* more reasonable that I should have put the things in her drawer than that Roberta should. As Julie would see it, I've got a nice, good, simple motive for wanting to get rid of her, but she isn't very bright and I don't think she'd ever be able to grasp Roberta's reason."

"All the same, remember Roberta isn't a fool. She can be astonishingly shrewd. And she's a relatively rich woman. Justin had an extraordinary number of aunts and uncles who died off one by one and left him their money, and it's mounted up gradually to quite a substantial amount. Also, Roberta's an invalid of the kind who might easily lose the will to live, now that she's lost Justin. I should say it's almost inevitable that anyone who comes to take care of her is going to start wondering about her will." He paused, tapped a few keys on the typewriter, frowned at what he had written and obliterated it with a row of x's. "I suppose you couldn't be persuaded to stay, Camilla?"

She shook her head decisively, "Not for much longer."

He gave her a thoughtful look, "A man, is it?"

"It's a lot of things. Among others, you're right, of course, I couldn't live long with Roberta without our coming to blows. And I know that isn't nice of me, but I'm not a particularly nice person."

"No? I'm glad to have it from the horse's mouth. I've been wondering about you a good deal these last few weeks. Just what you are, apart from being charming and intelligent and very self-controlled."

Camilla was not sure that she liked that self-controlled. It did not sound as if it were meant to be a compliment.

"Just what are you, Matthew, if it comes to that?" she asked.

"Well, if I ever get this damned thing finished——" he tapped the sheets of manuscript on the table beside him,

"— it ought to tell you. But it's extraordinary how much easier it seems to be to live a life than write it. D'you remember how Moira used to want me to write it, or get it on to tape, so that she could ghost it? She used to swear it'd be a sure-fire best-seller."

"Perhaps it still will be."

"Without Moira?" He gave a mirthless laugh and Camilla was sorry she had spoken so stupidly.

Moira Frensham had been a writer. She had been a prolific producer of fairly amusing, unselfconsciously romantic novels. She had discovered the knack of writing these during her often lonely days in some of the wilder parts of Kenya and Uganda and if her books had never been quite in the best-seller class, still, for a time, she and Matthew had been almost wealthy. Now his small pension was still eked out by a trickle of royalties coming from the sale of her paperbacks, but with no new Moira Frenshams being published, these were gradually disappearing from the bookstalls. So it was among Matthew's misfortunes that a good deal of his income had gone soon after the loss of his wife.

Not that he seemed to feel the lack of money. He lived his quiet life, with only a small car and no servant, saw a few friends, played a good deal of golf up at Santo da Serra, looked after his garden, cooked astonishingly well, and, when the bad patches came, settled down to writing his book.

All the same, Camilla thought a few minutes later, as she was walking back down the hill to Roberta's house, she hardly ever came away from a talk with Matthew without a curious sense of dissatisfaction with him. There was a futility about him that depressed her. He was frittering his life away as if he were already an old man. It fretted her, because, in spite of what he had said about her self-control, she was actually a person who could make very little sense of life except in terms of energy and passion. The passion might be for another person, or for work, or religion, or even for far less estimable things, but it had to be intense and all-absorbing and demanding to gain her understanding.

Meanwhile, however, it seemed as if the only thing for her to do was after all what Matthew had advised, send Julie Davy home and reconcile herself to staying on at least a little longer until a replacement for Julie could be found. And the quickest way of finding a replacement might be to telephone Christopher in London. Christopher Peters had connections, was efficient, and wanted Camilla to come home. If anyone could help to speed things up at the moment, he could. Camilla turned in under the vine-covered trellis that shaded the path to Roberta's door, meaning to go straight to the telephone.

But Roberta was standing just inside the door, supported by her crutches, her knuckles white as she grasped them, her blue eyes even more staring than usual.

"Where have you been?" she demanded excitedly. "You shouldn't go off like that without telling me where you're going."

"I only went to see Matthew," Camilla answered.

"Why?"

"Oh, just to talk." She had not yet decided what to say to Roberta about the viciousness of the trick that she had played on Julie. For Roberta, after all, was ill, was in a state of shock from Justin's death, and far from normal. "I didn't mean to be gone long. And Julie and Ione are here with you."

"Julie isn't here," Roberta said. "I don't know what you said when you talked to her, but a few minutes after you'd gone she went out too. Ione saw her go. She said Julie had just thrown on some clothes and hadn't done her hair and her face was terrible, and she went dashing off down the hill as if she'd gone out of her mind. Whatever did you say to her? I've got the most awful feeling that something dreadful is going to happen. And it'll be all your fault. I told you, I told you, I didn't want you to be horrid to her!"

However, nothing very dreadful happened that evening. About three hours passed, then Julie returned. Camilla heard the slip-slop of her sandals on the waxed floor of the hall, then the decisive shutting, which was not quite a slam, of her bedroom door.

Camilla went to the door and knocked on it.

"It's all right," came the reply in a dead voice, "I'm going."

"Can I come in?" Camilla asked.

There was a pause, then Julie said, "I've told you I'm going. I've arranged everything. You've nothing to worry about. Leave me alone."

"Have you had anything to eat?"

"I've had all I want, thank you."

Camilla opened the door. Julie was packing. She had the two suitcases that she had brought with her open on the bed and was rapidly bundling her belongings into them. She stood still for a moment to give Camilla a blind stare, then went on as before, as if she were not in the room.

"Where are you going?" Camilla asked.

"Home."

"But you can't go to-night."

"I'm going to a pension for the night, then I'm catching the early flight to Lisbon in the morning. Luckily it wasn't fully booked."

"You needn't have done that."

"Do you stay on in places where you aren't wanted?"

"If we could talk . . ."

A filmy cocktail dress, which so far Julie had had no occasion to wear, got rolled into a ball and jammed into one of the cases.

"We've nothing to talk about. You want to get rid of me and you fixed it so that Mrs. Ellison should think the worst of me. Well, I'm going. Now I wish you'd leave me alone."

"I didn't . . ." But Julie's mistake could not be corrected without the blame for what had happened being laid fairly and squarely on Roberta's shoulders and Camilla had a squeamishness about doing that, a sort of reluctant loyalty.

"You could at least spend the night here," she said. "I'll drive you to the airport in the morning."

"Thank you, I've a taxi coming for me in half an hour. I don't need help."

Julie slammed the lid down on the suitcases and tried to fasten it, but some folds of a nylon dressing-gown were bulging out at the edges and the locks would not hold.

Suddenly irritated by her incompetence, Camilla elbowed her out of the way, emptied the suitcase on to the bed and started packing it again.

Taken by surprise, Julie stood back to let her do it, but then in a high, hysterical voice, cried, "Oh, you're so damned good at things! Even a thing like packing, so bloody good! Take this way of getting me sacked. Clean, quick, ruthless. You knew how I'd react, you knew I wouldn't put up a fight. It's so horribly clever."

"Nobody's sacked you," Camilla said. "I don't want you to leave like this."

"That's the clever part of it. You understood me well enough to know what I'd do if you made the sort of accusations you did, even if you couldn't prove them. I suppose I'm a very gutless sort of person. I've often been told I am. I suppose I ought to fight back when people attack me. But I don't, I can't, I hate fighting, I'd sooner just get out of the way. But that doesn't mean I haven't opinions of my own and that I don't despise the people who go for me."

There was some violence in the way that Camilla shook out the crumpled cocktail dress, refolded it and put it back into the suitcase. It hurt, being despised, even if there was not the precise justification for it that Julie believed.

"What about your money?" Camilla asked. "You're entitled to a month's pay."

"Oh no, I'm not!" There was almost a note of triumph in Julie's voice. "As you said, nobody's sacked me, I'm simply going of my own accord, so I'm not entitled to anything. That's clever too."

"Don't be a fool." The suitcase shut quite easily now. "I

don't know if my sister has that amount of money in the house this evening, but she'll give you a cheque, or send it after you, which ever you like, if you really insist on going now."

"Oh, I'm going."

Suddenly Camilla felt as sick at herself as at Roberta. "I wish you wouldn't, Julie. If we could all just calm down . . . Honestly, you know, I don't believe for a moment you ordered those things."

"Of course you don't, because you did it yourself. But why—why did you have to do something so beastly? If only you'd just told me you didn't want me . . ." All at once the defiance drained out of Julie's voice. It became shaky with the effort of holding back tears. "I don't know what you've got against me. If you're really afraid I'd try to get round your sister once you're gone, you're absolutely wrong about me. I like her—I liked you both so much —I'd just have done my very best for her. And I didn't intend to stay for ever and ever."

"Oh, you didn't?"

"No, I . . . Oh, I don't know. Perhaps I'd have stayed. In any case I'd never have left Mrs. Ellison in the lurch. I'd have stayed on till you found someone else."

"I see," Camilla said. "Now, about your pay . . ."

"Oh, give me a cheque," Julie said drearily. "I can't really afford not to take it."

"What will you do when you get home?"

"Stay with my brother for a bit, I expect, and look for another job—where I'm sure to run into some other horrible thing. I wonder what it is about me that makes it happen. Is there something wrong with me, d'you think?" She looked at Camilla in an almost friendly, placatory way.

"You've just had a lot of bad luck," Camilla said. "Now I'd better tell my sister you're going."

She found Roberta on the terrace. She was sitting with a book on her lap which it was too dark for her to read, and with her gaze on the hillside and the distant bay, all

28

dark now except for the familiar pattern of the lights of the town.

"She's going?" Roberta said. She sounded genuinely astonished and concerned. "Going now?"

"She's got a taxi coming for her," Camilla said, "and she's got a room in a pension for the night and a seat on the early flight to Lisbon to-morrow."

"Oh, Camilla, you have made a mess of things, haven't you?" Roberta said with a sigh. "I never meant you to drive the poor girl out into the night."

"Into the night, into the day, what's the difference? Meanwhile, will you write a cheque for her month's wages?"

"Yes. Yes, of course. But really—to go just like that! I don't know what you said to her, but still, it's a very hysterical way to behave. She must be unbalanced, don't you think? It rather proves there was something in my first impression of her."

"Some people just don't like being falsely accused of even quite small nasty things, they're funny that way."

Camilla fetched Roberta's handbag from the sitting-room, switched on the terrace light so that she could write the cheque, and took it to Julie.

She had finished her packing, had put on a light coat over her summer dress and tied a chiffon scarf over her hair. Her momentary friendliness had gone. Her attractive face was cold and sullen. Taking the cheque without speaking, she folded it and put it into her handbag, checked her passport and ticket, then, refusing help, picked up her suitcases and carried them to the door and out on to the path under the vines to wait for the taxi.

It came a few minutes later. Without saying good-bye to Camilla, she got into it and was driven away.

By then Camilla found it an immense relief to see her go. Closing the door after her, she tried to settle down calmly to wait for her call to London to go through. She had been told, when she had tried to telephone Christopher earlier in the evening, that it would take some time, and

29

although she had guessed that it would, being told so induced a mood of frantic irritation. To have made up her mind that she must speak to him, and then not to be able to do so instantly, felt intolerable. It was a too bitter reminder of all those other times when she had known that he was within arm's length of his telephone but that, in case Helen should hear her, he would only be angry if she were to call him, whatever her own need.

Helen, of course, might overhear them now, but it would not matter, since Camilla had an excellent alibi for this call. It was being made on behalf of Roberta, who needed Christopher's help. Which was a joke of sorts, considering the sort of things that Roberta had said about Christopher ever since Camilla had made the mistake of half-confiding in her about him, the sort of things that she would probably start saying now, as soon as she knew that Camilla was going to speak to him.

To arm herself before Roberta got started, Camilla went to the drinks tray in the sitting-room and poured out an extra large whisky for herself. When she appeared with it on the terrace, Roberta observed at once, "You know, you drink too much. I've been noticing it. It rather worries me."

The night air on the terrace was pleasantly cool, with a light breeze blowing in from the sea. The darkness was scented with the heavy fragrance of ginger lilies. Camilla sank back in the white wicker chair.

When it was obvious that she was not going to answer, Roberta added, "I think perhaps I'll have one too. I feel quite upset this evening. This whole affair . . ." She sighed and looked very pained.

Camilla got up and fetched her a drink, then settled down to wait for the ringing of the telephone.

They were both silent for a while, then Roberta went on, "I suppose there's no doubt she did order those things —I mean, that there wasn't some quite ordinary mistake or misunderstanding."

"It's a little late to start worrying about that now," Camilla said.

"But she must have done it, don't you think?" Roberta's tone was blandly innocent.

"Listen," Camilla said, "I've done your dirty work for you, I've been your hatchet man, I've got rid of her. Now let's stop talking about it."

Roberta groaned. "Oh God, you're always so on edge nowadays. One can't discuss anything reasonably with you. And, I repeat, you *are* drinking too much."

"Not much more than you."

"Does it matter what I do? The sooner I'm out of things, the better." Roberta half-emptied her glass in a long swallow. "But at your age you shouldn't need it. About Julie, Camilla, suppose we made a mistake, there isn't any risk she could take some action against us, is there? For wrongful dismissal or something."

"She wasn't dismissed, she went of her own accord."

"But if by any chance it was all a mistake . . ."

"It was a very bad mistake, Roberta. A grisly one. You shouldn't have done it."

Roberta raised her delicately shaped eyebrows. "*I* shouldn't have . . . ?"

"Ordered the things and planted them in her drawer."

"I? You think *I* did that?" Roberta's voice went high and scandalised.

"I'm certain you did," Camilla said, "but it's all right, I let her go off thinking I wanted to get rid of her in case she gained undue influence over you and you cut me out of your will."

"You didn't!"

"I did. It seemed easier than trying to explain your motives to her."

"Motives? What motives? I haven't any motives!" Roberta cried it out wildly to the darkness round them. "What *is* one to do with you? I wish I understood what's really wrong. It's something to do with that man, I know.

31

I believe you're still clinging to the belief he'll leave his wife for you. But they don't, you know—not if they don't do it pretty soon after you come into their lives. Give it time, and home and family nearly always win. And you know he isn't to be trusted after what he did to you years ago —and what he's doing to his wife now. So if you're thinking that by becoming his mistress it would force his hand—or has that happened already? I do wish you'd tell me."

Camilla yawned. All at once she was very tired. It was a great strain, waiting for the telephone to ring.

"As a matter of fact, it hasn't," she said.

"Why not?"

"I'm not sure. I think it's just that I'm scared."

"That doesn't sound like you."

"I know, it's very odd. To love a person and yet be scared of him."

"Oh, scared of *him*. I thought you meant of the situation."

"No, I suppose that will sort itself out in its own way sooner or later." Tiredness, stress and the whisky were making Camilla feel more communicative than usual. "But in some queer way, he scares me now. He never did in the old days. It's something new in him, and I don't know what it is or why I feel it. I don't feel it when I'm actually with him, it's in between whiles . . . And if you want to know the rest of it, I believe you're right, whatever I do, home and family's going to win. But that doesn't necessarily solve my problem for me, does it?"

She was surprised to see sympathy in Roberta's eyes.

"I don't know—perhaps not. Of course, I understand he's the reason you've never married . . . And at least I'm sure now that coming here was the best thing that could have happened to you in the circumstances. It's giving you time to think seriously before you take any too drastic step. I'm glad, because I've felt selfish, letting you stay on when you were obviously eaten up with your own worries. But now I'm absolutely certain the best thing you can do is to stay till you've really cleared things up in your mind."

"Only the thinking you do when you're away from a man may not amount to much when you come face to face with him again. By the way, I'm expecting a call from him this evening. I'm going to ask him to help us find a replacement for Julie."

Roberta's hand jerked so sharply that some of her whisky spilled on to her dress.

"Oh, you're mad, you're mad!" she said. "For God's sake give him up before you've thrown your whole life away. Look for someone who'll care for you as you deserve. As Justin did for me. Christopher Peters isn't the only man in the world. He isn't the only man who'll ever love you. You're a very attractive woman, Camilla—you are, you know, though sometimes I think you don't realise it. You don't seem to understand the way that men react to you. If only you'd forget this wretched Christopher——"

The telephone began to ring.

But it was not Christopher. It was Matthew Frensham, ringing up to ask what, if anything, had been decided about Julie Davy. Camilla told him that Julie herself had decided what was to be done and had gone.

"I see, and you're staying on for the present," he said. "Roberta's skeleton staff—and all she really wants."

"What else can I do?"

"Well, speaking for myself, I'm very glad," he said, "but I'm sorry because I know you wanted to get away."

"I'll manage." Camilla was conscious only of impatience, wanting him to get off the line as quickly as possible, in case the call to London should go through. "Thanks for ringing, Matthew. Good night."

"I was going to say, I'll be over to-morrow to take Roberta for a drive, if she wants to go," he said.

"That's nice of you. Thank you."

"And let me know if there's any other way I can help to let you off the hook from time to time while you're waiting for someone to come instead of Julie."

"Thank you."

"And don't get too depressed."

"No. Good night."

"Good night." He rang off and Camilla returned to her drink.

It was not until nearly midnight that the telephone rang again. Camilla had helped Roberta to bed, had closed and locked the door on to the terrace, gone to her bedroom and was in her dressing-gown, trying uselessly to read, when the ringing of the bell brought her off her bed with a bound. This time it was Christopher's voice that spoke, sounding, from far away, close to her ear and clear and very startled.

"Cam?" He was almost the only person who ever called her that and she had never quite made up her mind whether or not she liked it. "What's happened? Is something wrong?"

He had a pleasant, incisive voice, light and quiet. He never had to raise it to be heard. It matched his kind of under-emphasised, almost unnoticeable good looks. He was thirty, about Camilla's own height, slight and dark, with a pointed face and rather sharp, regular features, which might have looked ascetic but for a gleam of recklessness in his eyes. All the same, Camilla had sometimes thought, perhaps there were traces of the ascetic in him which would dominate his character in the end, though only when he had tried everything else. They were not a noticeable part of him at present.

"Are you alone?" she asked.

She thought that he must be or he would have used a different tone of voice when he spoke her name. Helen thought, or was believed by them to think, that the relationship between them was a purely business one.

"Yes, as it happens, I am," he said. "Helen and the children have gone to the sea for a week. Cam, when are you coming back?"

"Soon. I——"

"Come now. Don't wait."

"I can't."

"You can. All you've got to do is make your mind up and come."

34

"No, it isn't. There've been complications. I've got to stay on at least for a time."

"You haven't. You could come to-morrow if you wanted to. Why don't you? You've been away much too long already, longer than I can stand. Please come back."

"Do let me talk, Christopher. I didn't ring up to talk about that. There *have* been complications. The girl who was to have stayed with Roberta and looked after her has —well, changed her mind and gone."

"She's what? Gone?" He cursed explosively, then added, "Well, I don't blame her. I don't see anyone standing Roberta for long, to go by what you've told me."

"Justin did."

"He was a saint, by all accounts. Cam, please come back. I'm getting scared you aren't ever going to come back. I mean it. I lost you once by being a fool, and now I have horrible attacks of feeling sure I'm never going to see you again. And I want to be sure that's crazy. Please hurry back, darling Cam. I'm a nearly crazy man."

"Please, Christopher, let me tell you why I rang up." She heard her own voice tremble and wondered how clearly it carried on the telephone. "I can't come till I've found someone to stay with Roberta and I thought perhaps you could help me. You meet such a lot of people and some of them must have daughters or sisters, or even mothers or grandmothers, who'd love the chance of a prolonged visit to Madeira. Can't you find someone for us?"

"Cam, just say once you love me," he said. "You ring me up from a world away and you don't even bother to say you love me. Say it, then we'll talk about this other thing."

She drew an unsteady breath. "Oh God, of course I love you."

"Say it without the 'of course.' That makes it sound a bit threadbare—ready to fall apart in rags and tatters at any moment. And say you're coming back soon. I mean, really soon."

"Christopher, I love you and I'm coming back as soon as I can. Now about this girl——"

"If you don't come soon, I'm coming to fetch you."

"But can you do this thing for me?" she asked.

"I'll do my best," he said. "I'll ask around."

He could ask his friends and his customers and ask them to ask their friends and their customers. Christopher owned three small, exceedingly successful restaurants in London, each of which he had built up from practically nothing to something very special. It was when he had employed Camilla to paint a mural for one of these that they had met again after an interval of seven years.

It had not been a chance meeting. He had seen some work of hers in an exhibition, had written to her, saying that he might have a commission for her if she wanted it, and suggesting that they might meet to discuss it. She had gone, believing that she was cured of him, mainly out of curiosity. And she had found, of course, that she was not cured at all, and that neither, apparently, was he. But he was married, with two children, a state of affairs which Camilla had not found herself able to overlook.

Christopher had not started life in the restaurant business. He had left Oxford with a degree in Medieval French, and when Camilla had first met him and they had fallen in love, he had been wondering restlessly whether to teach, the thought of which he hated, go into his family's textile business in Leeds, which appalled him quite as much, or perhaps become a mechanic in a garage or take to the sea. He had been far too immature and unsettled for marriage. But Camilla, at twenty-one, had not understood that, and presently he had dropped abruptly out of her life with a girl who had. Helen had come into his life about three years later, and it had been with five thousand pounds which she had inherited from her mother that they had bought their first restaurant.

It had been a shabby little café, barely more than a fish-and-chip shop, but now it was difficult to obtain a meal there for less than three pounds. As business partners the relationship between Christopher and Helen was excellent. They both had a flair for the work that they had chosen, were extremely hard workers, trusted each other's judgment and were ready to face the same sort of risks together. But if they had ever been in love, it had been short-lived, at least on Christopher's side. His children had a hold on his emotions, but not Helen. Or so he said. Just as in the past, Camilla had discovered during the few months since she had started seeing him again, it was advisable to take a good deal of what he said with a pinch of salt.

In some things he was reliable. She knew that she could trust him when he went on now, "If I can't find anyone, I'll advertise and vet the applications for you, if any. But as a matter of fact, I'm beginning to have an idea already about someone who might be just what you want. It's a little late to get in touch with her to-night, but I'll ring her up first thing in the morning."

"Please do that," Camilla said.

"I will, I promise."

That promise he would keep. As a man of business he had had to learn not to be casual about such things.

But when he went on to say once more, "And remember, if you don't come back soon, I'm coming to fetch you," Camilla knew that it was a different matter.

As they said good night to one another and she put the telephone down, she thought with a pang that it would really give her the surprise of her life if he came to Madeira.

CHAPTER III

WITH UNCANNY SPEED, as he did so many things, Christopher found a young woman who was most eager to take a job in Funchal.

He described her in a letter to Camilla. Joanne Willis had been the secretary of a friend of his for the past six years, an excellent secretary, and the friend was very sad at the thought of losing her, but some sort of trouble had developed recently in her home life and she badly wanted a change of job and scene. She was thirty-two and if she was not much to look at, she was even-tempered, reliable and intelligent.

Perhaps it was unfortunate that he wrote this to Camilla. It gave Roberta the opportunity of saying that since she was to be the employer of the woman, he might at least have had the courtesy to write to her, instead of treating her as a mental defective, whose opinions were of no account.

"It rather looks as if he isn't quite—well, doesn't exactly know how to do things, doesn't it?" she said with the light sneer that always had a way of coming into her voice when she spoke of anyone or anything of importance to Camilla, and which was nearly always successful in getting under Camilla's skin. "However, I suppose it's very good of him to have troubled. Such a busy man, I shouldn't have thought he would. But 'not much to look at'—what does that mean? Pimply and fat, with greasy, stringy hair? I tell you, if she's like that, she's going straight home again. I can't bear having hideous people round me."

"All right, I'll write and say she won't do," Camilla said.

"Oh no, no, not when he's been so kind." Roberta had the knack of making the word "kind" sound as if it were some peculiarly unpleasant vice. "I'd hate him to think I was discourteous or unappreciative. But 'Joanne'—what a name! I suppose she's really Joan or Jane, but thought she'd improve on things."

So it was arranged that Joanne Willis should come to Funchal and on a Saturday afternoon, ten days after Julie Davy had left, Camilla drove out to the airport, about twenty kilometres on the other side of the town, to meet the newcomer.

The clouds had hung low on the mountains all that day, but in the late afternoon they lifted, and although they still obscured the peaks, as they did for most of the time at that time of the summer, they left the high green slopes, where an unlikely mixture of pine and mimosa grew together, in sunshine.

As Camilla drove along the winding road between hills and sea, she tried to make plans, on the assumption that Roberta and Joanne Willis would suit one another. Not that this seemed likely. Roberta had obviously made up her mind to dislike the woman, and however competent and willing she might turn out to be, it seemed probable that some reason would soon be found for getting rid of her. Then they would be back to the beginning and while they advertised again, or appealed to friends for help, and found another girl who wanted to come here but who again would be found wanting, a week would slide by, a fortnight, a month . . .

A depressing lassitude possessed Camilla. During these ten days of doing almost everything for Roberta, of helping her to dress and undress, which actually she could just manage alone, but which took her a painfully long time; of helping her to get into her bath and out of it; of fetching and carrying for her and fully realising the extent of her helplessness, it had begun to seem as if there could never be any escape. It had also begun to seem occasionally as if perhaps there was no real point in escaping.

That really scared Camilla. The problem of Christopher apart, what sort of cabbage would she become if she stayed on and on?

Cabbages were an important export of this island. They grew in enormous quantities on the terraced slopes of the mountains, looking perfectly charming in rows of lovely blue-green bud-like shapes in those smooth little pockets of red-brown soil, one above the other, on the steep hillsides. But there was a limit to the imaginative appeal of a cabbage. It would never burst into riotous bloom, or bear exciting fruit, but would only run raggedly and unattractively to seed, if it were not harvested in time and dispatched to some cooking-pot.

A roar in the air told Camilla that the plane was approaching. Only a few minutes after she had reached the airport, and making the intolerable screaming sound of the big jets when they land, it taxied along the narrow air-strip that had been carved out of the hillside. She waited in the car until she saw the first passengers straggling out from the airport building, then she got out of the car and walked towards the entrance.

She thought that it would be quite easy for her to spot an Englishwoman of thirty-two, travelling alone. Yet when Joanne Willis emerged from the building, Camilla almost missed her. For Miss Willis was not alone. She was with a man and Camilla took them for a couple, arriving together. But then the man said a quick, formal good-bye, as from one stranger to another, and made for the line of taxis, while the woman remained standing alone, looking around her.

There was something vaguely familiar to Camilla about the man. He was tall and rather bony, with a slightly shambling walk, a pointed face, large ears and dark hair with a tinge of red in it. The feeling that she had seen him before would have made her think that she had seen him about in the town, if his skin had not had the pallor of a newcomer's. But believing that he was no concern of hers, she forgot him and approached the woman, who was fending off a hotel tout who had a hand on her suitcase and was trying to persuade her towards a taxi.

"Miss Willis?" Camilla said.

"Yes. Are you Miss Carey?" The woman had a cool, confident voice and an air of casual composure with no trace of shyness in it. "Could you please tell this character to let me alone? I've been trying to explain to him I was being met, but he doesn't seem to understand."

But the man had now realised that there was no profit to be had here and was walking off, looking for other prey.

"I've a car here," Camilla said. "Come along. Is this all your luggage?"

Miss Willis had one moderate-sized, blue fibreglass suitcase and a little overnight bag.

"Yes, I always travel light."

She looked rather hot, tired and crumpled from travelling, yet Christopher had not been fair to her, Camilla thought, in saying that she was not much to look at. Certainly Joanne Willis might not catch the eye in a crowd, but she was neatly built, her light brown hair was glossy and thick, she had big, light brown eyes with flecks of gold in them, and a smooth, oval face with excellent skin. It was a plumpish face, a little blank and expressionless, but on the whole amiable-looking, with a placid, good-natured smile on the full, slightly pouting lips.

Yet a curious thing happened to Camilla just before she picked up the suitcase and they started towards the car. For an instant she was aware of an acute antagonism to the other woman, of a sharp recoil from her, a sense of intense distrust.

It was much the same as Roberta's description of her feeling on first meeting Julie Davy. And as Roberta's feeling had, Camilla's lasted only for a moment. By the time that the suitcase was in the boot and she and Joanne Willis were in the car, the discomfort had gone, and in only a few minutes Camilla had begun to feel thankful for the new-comer's self-assurance, for the hint of toughness about her. This might be just what Roberta needed. She might even, you never could tell, like it for a change.

On the way into Funchal Camilla did her best to tell Miss Willis something about the country through which they were driving, naming the little villages of Santa Cruz and Canico, then pointing out, in the town, the Governor's palace, the square red and white tower of the fifteenth-century cathedral with the little candle-snuffer steeple on top, the statue of Zarco, the discoverer of Madeira, the Botanic Garden.

Miss Willis did not say much in reply. She did not exclaim, as Julie Davy had when she arrived, at the beauty of a flame-tree, covered in a blaze of blossom, or the jacarandas waving over the deep ravine under the Ponte Monumental. But she was interested in some of the new hotels, saying that they looked pretty good, and that she hadn't realised that they'd have modern places like that here. She also seemed surprised at the number of cars, almost as if she had expected to find the inhabitants going about in bullock carts. Camilla soon came to the conclusion that Miss Willis had never been abroad before, or if she had, then it had probably been on a tour, on which she had thought it far more important to notice her fellow-travellers than the country that they had happened to be visiting.

A tour of this kind was in the town at the moment. There was a cruise-ship in the harbour, and its passengers, in groups, were strolling along the streets, their faces red and sweaty from the unaccustomed heat and in their arms a booty of basket work, embroideries and bottles of Madeira.

Joanne Willis noticed them too and said, "Have you ever been on a cruise, Miss Carey? I'd just love to go on one. I don't think there's anything I'd like more. I'd like all the different sorts of people you'd meet and the dancing and clothes and having fun."

"I'm afraid you aren't going to find it a lot of fun looking after my sister," Camilla said. "I do hope you understood that when you decided to come."

"Oh, I only said I liked having fun, I didn't say I couldn't get on without it," Joanne Willis answered laconically. "And I don't believe in kidding myself. I know what I like, but also what I can afford. It doesn't break my heart if they aren't the same. Of course I don't know how good I'll be, looking after an invalid. I'm not used to it, but I'll do my best. It's been luck for me, getting a chance like this to get away from home. Things have been a bit difficult there lately."

"The work isn't hard, it's just that you've got to be on call most of the time," Camilla told her.

"Well, I shan't mind that."

"And the British community here are mostly fairly elderly, retired people, and I don't think it's very easy to get to know the Portuguese, though perhaps it's just that my sister hasn't tried very hard. After four years here, she only speaks a few words of the language."

"Well, I could never manage the language either, so I don't suppose that'll worry me," said Joanne.

"I'm just telling you the worst," Camilla said. "The other side of it is the climate's marvellous and there's some good swimming. And with the car you can get up into the mountains, where there are some wonderful walks."

"I'm not much of a one for walking," said Joanne Willis. "Swimming's fine, though, and lying around in the sun. Do you suppose Mrs. Ellison and I are going to get on?"

"Why not?" Camilla stopped the car at Roberta's door and got out. "Here we are. Come in and meet her."

They found Roberta on the terrace, with Matthew Frensham. He stood up when Camilla and Joanne appeared and Joanne's gaze went to him quickly and curiously before it went to Roberta. When it did turn to Roberta and Roberta's met it, the two of them sized one another up in a long, neutral glance. Then Roberta held out a hand, smiled one of her more brilliant smiles and told Joanne how glad she was to see her, said that she hoped that she had had a pleasant journey and that she would be happy here.

Having expected a far chillier greeting, Camilla was pleasantly surprised, although she knew that this warmth of itself did not mean much. All her life Roberta had worked hard at charming strangers, any strangers, from celebrities whom chance brought in her way, to waiters in restaurants and station porters, and part of how she did it was to appear immensely charmed by them. Generally it was only after several meetings that it became possible to guess how she really felt about a person.

She had changed for this meeting with Joanne into a dress of white wild silk, cut very plainly, her pearls and her antique turquoise and diamond ear-rings, so it was evident that she had determined to make an impressive first appearance.

"But you're so young!" she went on, still smiling up at Joanne, who in her travel-rumpled state, was looking every one of her thirty-two years. "You look far younger than I expected. I'm afraid you're going to find us terribly boring.

I wonder what made a girl like you think of coming to a job like this."

"Oh, don't worry, I shan't be bored," Joanne said in her laconic way. "I don't often get bored. Could I have a bath, please? I feel sticky."

"Why, of course. My sister will show you your room. But perhaps you'd like a drink first. Matthew, if you'd fetch the drinks——"

"No thanks, I'd sooner have the bath first, if that's all right," Joanne said positively.

Roberta faintly raised her eyebrows at such early opposition, but said as amicably as before, "Of course—but join us here when you're ready. Then you must tell us more about yourself. I'm curious, I'd really like to know why you wanted this job. You aren't what I was expecting."

"Well, I hope I'll do," said Joanne.

"I'm sure you will. I'm sure you and I are going to get on very well."

"Just tell me what you want and I'll always do my best."

"I know. I saw at one glance that that's the sort of person you are."

"And I don't mind being told off either. I'm used to that at home."

"Oh, I'm sure I shan't have to do much of that." Roberta laughed. "I'm really not at all a difficult person to get along with. Am I, Matthew?"

He refrained from answering and Camilla led Joanne away to her room.

A few minutes later Camilla returned to the terrace, having shown Joanne the little room that had been Julie Davy's, and the bathroom. Matthew had fetched a tray of drinks and was pouring them out.

"A young woman who knows her own mind," he remarked.

"Which is so refreshing," said Roberta. "She hasn't the awful, wilting, trodden-on air of that other girl. I think I'm going to like her."

"I never noticed Julie doing any wilting till you did some treading." Camilla took the glass that Matthew held out to her. "If I had to choose between the two, I'd take Julie."

"That's just snobbery, my dear," said Roberta. "Julie had a better background, obviously, a better accent and better manners. This girl's decidedly a bit brash, but perhaps one can do something about that. And I feel instinctively that she's good and honest, not a slimy little snake-in-the-grass, like that other one."

"I don't think you'll do anything with her that she doesn't want you to do," said Matthew. He looked at Camilla. "What do you think? Will it work?"

"I suppose if Roberta wants it to, it may," she said.

"You don't sound hopeful," he said.

"My dears, I'm going to make it work if it kills me," Roberta exclaimed, banging on the ground with one of her crutches. "I know Camilla can't stand me much longer without going round the bend, but she's got such a sense of duty she won't go away till I positively send her. And, God, how I hate being a duty! How I *hate* it! Oh, I'm going to make this work."

A remark which might have reassured Camilla if she had thought for a moment of taking it seriously.

But intent, apparently, on carrying out her resolution when presently Joanne reappeared after her bath, Roberta said she hoped that she felt better now, told her what a charming dress she was wearing, how well that shade of pale blue suited her, and how prettily she had done her hair.

In fact, the dress was commonplace and shapeless and it neither fitted nor suited Joanne particularly well, and she had screwed her mouse-brown hair up into a peculiar plume of curls, which only exaggerated the plumpness of her features. But Roberta was convinced that flattery was the quickest way to anyone's heart, and the fact that she thought it worth while to go on flattering Joanne might be a hopeful sign.

"And now tell me," Roberta went on, when Joanne was

45

settled in a chair with a glass of dry Madeira, "what did make you think of coming to this job? You were a secretary, so we heard from Mr. Peters."

"That's right," said Joanne.

"But surely that was a much better and more interesting job than this. It's a rather old-fashioned-sounding job, isn't it, being a companion to an invalid?"

"The sort only the half-witted go for—yes, I know," said Joanne. "But I liked the idea of coming abroad when Mr. Peters suggested it."

"He suggested it to you?"

"Well, in a way."

"You know him quite well then?" Roberta flicked an equivocal little glance at Camilla which Camilla pretended not to have observed.

"My boss knows him quite well," Joanne answered, "and he knew I wanted to get away. My boss, I mean. He's always been very good to me and he knew I wanted to get away from home. My father married again, you see, and my stepmother hadn't much use for a grown-up daughter around the place. I don't blame her. I dare say I'd be the same in her shoes. She's a couple of years younger than me."

"Ah, now I understand," Roberta said. "I know just how you feel. I was once in much the same position myself. Not as old as you, actually, so I couldn't simply leave home, but how I wanted to! Oh, I'm glad you told me that. I do understand so completely."

"I don't dislike her, you know," Joanne said equably. "She used to be my best friend, as a matter of fact."

"But that must make it far harder."

"Oh, I don't know. I dare say we'd have got along all right if we'd had to. But I kind of thought it'd be fairer to everyone if I got out of the way. And of course I've always wanted to travel."

"So you'll be travelling on from here quite soon, I suppose."

"That'll depend a good deal on how you like me, won't it?"

"I'm sure I'm going to like you very much." Roberta turned a bright, smiling glance on Camilla and Matthew. "You know, I'm so relieved. You both know how nervous I am of strangers, but I understand Joanne's position so well and I do so admire her attitude to it. It's both realistic and generous and far more mature than mine ever was in similar circumstances. I'm sure everything is going to work out wonderfully."

"I'm very glad," Matthew said. "Now I'll be getting home."

He stood up to go. But just then the doorbell rang.

"I wonder who that is," Roberta remarked without much interest as they heard Ione's footsteps crossing the hall as she went to the door. "Now tell me, Joanne—you don't mind if I call you Joanne? And you must call me Roberta. Such an absurd name, isn't it? But for some reason I've never met anyone who thought of shortening it to Bobbie. Of course, I'd kill them if they did. But tell me, Joanne, what are your interests—apart from being the excellent secretary I'm sure you were? Music? Sport? Because I'm so anxious you shouldn't be bored."

In the hall Ione was speaking in Portuguese, then in faltering English. A man's voice answered her. Then, after a moment, she came out on to the terrace, bringing with her the tall man with the big ears and the dark chestnut hair with whom Camilla had seen Joanne Willis emerge from the airport. Ione made a brave but unsuccessful attempt to pronounce his name, then disappeared, leaving him standing in the doorway of the sitting-room.

He looked at each of them there in turn. It was plain that he was very angry, and his anger somehow made him look younger than the thirty that he probably was, because he did not look a man who was used to anger, or who knew how to handle it. He looked highly-strung, nervous, intelligent, the sort of man who might have flares of temper, of which later he would be deeply ashamed, but to whom intense and continuing anger, of the kind that smouldered now behind his eyes, would be not only a very painful but a bewildering experience. It gave him almost an air of innocence. It did not look any the less dangerous for that.

Camilla knew now why he had seemed familiar at the airport. It was not that she had ever seen him before, it was simply a case of a family resemblance. That reddish, curly hair, the grey eyes, the sharp chin . . .

Picking on Roberta as the person to address, he said in a jerky voice, "Mrs. Ellison? I'm Alec Davy. Julie Davy's my sister and I'm going to get an apology out of you, or make real trouble."

Roberta could be relied on never to lose her head or her poise in an awkward situation. Surveying him calmly, she replied in her pleasantest social tone, "Good evening, Mr. Davy." And with a gesture at the others on the terrace, "My sister, Miss Carey. Mr. Frensham. And Miss Willis, who's just arrived to take your sister's place."

He looked at Joanne. "You didn't tell me you were coming to these people," he said.

"You didn't ask me, did you?" she replied.

"If you had, I'd have warned you what sort of trap you were walking into," he said.

"Do you two know each other, then?" Roberta asked brightly, as if making the pleasant discovery that two old friends knew one another.

"We met on the plane from Lisbon," Joanne answered. "He didn't tell me anything about himself, except that he was coming here for a holiday."

She showed no pleasure at seeing Alec Davy again, yet no annoyance either. Her expression as she regarded him had no animation at all.

Roberta smiled at him charmingly. "And if I were you, Mr. Davy, that's just what I'd do. I'd have a nice holiday, and forget any unpleasantness between us. We've nothing against your sister, you know. If she hadn't rushed off as she did, without giving us a chance to talk things over, I'm sure we could have sorted everything out. So sit down and have a drink with us. Matthew, if you'd bring out another chair . . ."

But Alec Davy did not budge from the doorway of the sitting-room and Matthew did not trouble to go for the extra chair, or to pour out a drink. He had assessed the other man's mood more accurately than Roberta and was watching the scene between them with deep interest.

"Thank you, I haven't come for a drink," Alec Davy said. "I've come to tell you how shamefully I think you treated Julie and to insist—I repeat, to insist on an apology."

"An apology? Is that all? But of course I'll apologise," Roberta said. "I do apologise. There. Now do have that drink and let's all be friends."

"A *written* apology," the young man said.

"Oh, a written one . . ." Roberta's eyes became evasive. "But that's making an awfully serious thing of it."

"It *is* awfully serious."

"No, no, you mustn't take it like that," she said. "The whole thing was a misunderstanding and that's all it was. My sister misunderstood me and was far too blunt with Julie, and Julie, as I told you, took offence and rushed away without giving us a chance to talk things over. All my fault really, I admit it, because I ought to have taken care that my sister didn't misunderstand me."

He turned for the first time to take a careful look at Camilla. He was hating every minute of this, she thought, but had set himself a task which he intended to carry through to the end. "Miss Carey, were you the one who actually accused Julie of trying to buy things on Mrs. Ellison's account?"

"No," she said. "I didn't accuse her of anything."

"She told me a Miss Carey had deliberately tried to turn Mrs. Ellison against her."

"She was quite wrong," Camilla said. "I spoke to her,

when my sister asked me to, about the things that had been ordered, but I didn't accuse her of anything and I wasn't trying to turn my sister against her."

"Of course not," Roberta said. "I liked Julie and I hoped she'd be happy here and stay with me. She was simply hopelessly over-sensitive."

"She *is* sensitive," he agreed. "She's very highly emotional. But that's no reason——"

"Perhaps," Roberta interrupted, "it was because of that other horrid thing, the thing at the school, that she'd been involved in. And you must admit, it wasn't quite fair to keep it from us that she'd had another job before she came here, was it? When we found out, it helped to create an atmosphere of distrust. If she'd told us the truth at the start, we'd probably all have got on far better."

A dull red coloured Alec Davy's face. "I told her that myself, but she didn't listen to me. That other damned business had left too much of a scar. All the same, to have it happen *twice*——! That's why I came. If it hadn't been for that first time, I'd have told her to forget the whole business here, but she's right on the edge of a nervous breakdown as a result of this rotten thing you've done to her, and I promised her that I wouldn't come home without that written apology."

"Now wait a minute——" It was Matthew, but Roberta interrupted him with an excited glitter in her eyes.

"No, no, Matthew, leave this to me. Let him say what he wants. I like to find a man who's ready to charge about the earth, righting other people's wrongs. I like it enormously. Mr. Davy, I like you and I do wish you'd sit down and have that drink with us while we talk things over."

"I shouldn't press the drinks on him, if I were you, Mrs. Ellison," Joanne said, making a slightly wry face over a sip of her own Madeira. "He had enough on the plane to last him for quite a while. Stoking up for this scene, I suppose."

"Well, if you won't," said Roberta, "will you just tell

me this, Mr. Davy? What's the truth about the very expensive cosmetics I found in your sister's drawer? If she didn't buy them, how did they get there?"

Camilla wanted to stop her. This man was not a fool and he might easily stumble on the awkward truth. But he was looking at Camilla again, the slow-burning, steady anger still smouldering on behind his grey eyes.

"I think Julie must have been right," he said. "I think Miss Carey ordered the things and put them in Julie's room and somehow hinted to you, Mrs. Ellison, that they were there. You asked Miss Carey to handle the matter for you, and she did it on purpose in such a way as to get rid of Julie. I can only suppose she was afraid she might lose some of her own influence with you. That's the only explanation that makes sense."

You can stand only just so much injustice, Camilla found. Suddenly she lost her temper.

"Oh, if you're looking for an explanation that makes sense," she said, "you won't find any explanation at all! None of us, and that includes your sister, Mr. Davy, has behaved at all sensibly over this."

Matthew hurriedly cleared his throat.

"As a matter of fact, I believe I've an explanation of what really happened," he said.

"Ah, the policeman," Roberta said. "Always solving things. Isn't that nice? Go ahead, my dear."

"Well," Matthew said, "I think these cosmetics were sent here by accident in the first place. They'd been ordered by someone else as a present for someone or other but got sent here with some of Mrs. Ellison's medicines and put on her bill by mistake. And Miss Davy undid the parcel, and found these things packed in that gift-wrapping stuff, probably with something written on them that made her think they were meant for her——"

"She did think they were a present for her, but not because of any gift-wrapping," her brother said. "It was because she found them in her drawer."

"Well, don't you think that might be where she

misled you a little?" Matthew suggested. "Don't you think she may have been so embarrassed when she found out they weren't meant for her at all that she got in a muddle about why she'd ever thought they were? Not intentionally. Perhaps she simply got confused and by then really couldn't remember exactly how it happened."

Alec Davy only grinned sardonically. "You're a policeman, Mr. Frensham?"

"I once was."

"You've probably had a lot more practice then in tracking down the guilty, than at sloshing whitewash around."

"It's a reasonable explanation——"

"Reasonable!" Alec Davy's big ears reddened to their pointed tips. "It's simple-minded idiocy. I'm sticking to Julie's explanation for the moment, which is that Miss Carey deliberately blackened my sister's character to discredit her with Mrs. Ellison. And I'm staying here till I get a written apology from them both. I'm not going home without it."

At last he had got under Roberta's skin. "And a reference, perhaps," she suggested venomously, "to go with those two so explicit ones she sent to me?"

"What references?" he asked.

"The one from your uncle, the bishop, and the one from the head of her college."

"I don't know what you're talking about," he said. "I haven't got an uncle who's a bishop." Abruptly he turned on Joanne Willis. "And you—you've heard all this, your eyes must be open now, you know the kind of place you've come to. I hope you've grasped the moral. Don't let Mrs. Ellison like you too much, or Miss Carey will take steps to get rid of you. But if she does, if you find anything you can't account for among your belongings —cosmetics, or perhaps something more dramatic next time, jewellery, or money—if you get into any trouble, you can count on me to help you. I'm staying at the Vila Angela. You'll find me there until further notice."

He turned and shambled out through the sitting-room.

"Well, well, no bishop," Matthew said. "That's interesting."

There was silence for a moment, then Roberta began to laugh.

"I must say, I think I carried that off rather well," she said. "Won't someone congratulate me? And I was right about Julie, wasn't I? Faked references on top of everything else—and the poor young man didn't even seem to know it."

Nobody answered.

Suddenly Camilla realised that Matthew was looking intently at Joanne and she glanced at her too to see what there was about her that so absorbed him.

Certainly the expression on Joanne's face was startling. For if it was not panic that shone blankly in her eyes, Camilla did not know what it was. Joanne looked like a terrified creature caught in a trap, or someone unable to swim, helpless in deep water.

But as soon as she saw that both Matthew and Camilla were watching her, she lowered her eyelids, got up and said quietly, "Excuse me—I'd like to finish my unpacking."

Moving slowly at first, but then hurrying, she disappeared into the house.

"An odd young woman," Matthew observed. "You know, Roberta, I'm not sure that I take to her much. I've a very uneasy feeling she isn't quite what she seems."

"Now, isn't that just like you?" Roberta exclaimed indignantly. "Oh God, why are people so perverse? Just because I've decided I do like her, you have to decide you don't. I think there's something very attractive about her, something straightforward and direct and rather earthy that I like very much."

"Didn't you see her face just now?"

"Her face? What's wrong with it? She's not at all bad-looking. When I've persuaded her to do something quite different about her hair and taught her a little about make-up, and stopped her ever wearing that ghastly shade of blue, you'll find she's very presentable."

"I didn't mean that."

"No, you meant the way she got scared at the way that young man was behaving. Of course I saw that. But just put yourself in Joanne's place, arriving here, a stranger, and straight away having a lunatic like that turn on you and tell you you've walked into some sort of mysterious trap. I'd have been scared myself. In fact, I *was* scared. He's as unbalanced as his sister."

"All right," Matthew said. "All right, all right, let's not argue."

His voice spoke of an utter weariness of arguments with Roberta.

It annoyed Camilla. She held all kinds of things against Roberta herself, old grudges that she would never forget, old jealousies and present irritations, but if anyone else showed symptoms of a state of mind like hers, she started feeling a prickly protectiveness towards her sister.

"I think perhaps I'd better go and have a chat with Joanne." Roberta was slowly levering herself out of her chair. It was a job in which she never liked to be helped. She reached for her crutches. "Just to make sure her room's all right and that she has everything she wants. Did you think of putting any flowers in her room, Camilla?"

"I put some marigolds there this morning."

"Good. Thank you. It's wonderful how you think of everything. I always feel myself there's nothing like a few flowers in one's bedroom for making one feel welcome." With a tapping of her crutches and her footsteps dragging, Roberta went into the house.

Matthew said, "I must be getting home."

But instead he sat down on the edge of a chair, rubbing the knuckles of his powerful hands together and frowning down at them.

The dusk was coming fast. It spread a lavender wash over the hillside, while the evening scents of the flowers in the garden below grew stronger. The narrow line of the Atlantic, visible beyond the rooftops, was dark, except for a few moving points of light, which meant fishing-boats putting out to sea.

One of the lights was far more brilliant and was moving faster than the others. It was probably another cruise-ship, like the one that Joanne and Camilla had seen in the harbour in the afternoon, arriving for a twenty-four hour visit to the island.

"Well, what do *you* think?" Matthew asked at last.

Camilla shrugged her shoulders.

He went on, "Not enormously taken, are you?"

"Not bowled over."

"What will you do then?"

"Go home or stay on, do you mean? I suppose I'll have to stay for a little and see how things work out."

He was still frowning down at his big, bony hands, not looking at Camilla. He looked like someone trying to remember something which he had known a moment ago, then had suddenly unaccountably forgotten. "There's something wrong with that young woman," he said. "I can't put a name to it. It's just a hunch, and they're tricky things, hunches. So tempting to take as gospel truth, just because they come out of nowhere. Revelations, so to speak. All the same, why should a quite good-looking young woman like that go to so much trouble to make herself as plain as possible?"

"Some people do that unintentionally," Camilla said.

"Oh yes, just because they've no taste, or they've had a puritanical upbringing, or something. Do you think that's her trouble?"

"It's early to say."

"And that manner of hers, a sort of calculated near-impudence, is that her normal manner?"

"Perhaps."

"Then it isn't the manner of a good secretary."

"No." That had already struck Camilla.

"Didn't you tell me she'd been someone's very valued secretary for six years? No, it won't do! There's something all wrong about her. And I don't mean just her excessive panic when Davy spoke about her having walked into a trap here. What else was it he said? Something about jewels, money . . ." He paused then suddenly drove one fist into the palm of his other hand. "That's it! That look—it's the look of someone who's really got something to hide, and the thing I was calling impudence—it's the boldness that covers that fear, the continuous, nagging sort of fear you get when you mustn't make a false step. It's a look I used to know so well. A woman gets it when her man's been arrested, or she thinks he's probably going to be arrested, and she doesn't know how much you really know about him. She gets terrified of saying just the one thing too much, yet she knows she may not have the strength of mind just to keep her mouth shut——"

"Oh, now wait, Matthew." Camilla was astonished at his mounting excitement. "Just because you haven't taken a liking to her, it doesn't mean she's a crook."

He grinned at her. "No, I was getting carried away. All the same, I'd very much like to know what her real reason was for wanting to leave home in such a hurry."

"What's wrong with the reason she gave us?" Camilla asked. "When my father married my mother, who was twenty years younger than he was, and left him three years later with a good-looking Australian engineer, Roberta would have left home on the spot if she'd been just a little older. What she said about that was quite true."

"All right then, but that friend of yours who found Miss Willis for you—do you think he really knows what sort of a secretary she was for those six years? In other words, does he really know anything about her?"

Naturally, Camilla had already wondered about this herself. Did Christopher know Joanne Willis personally, or had he simply grabbed at the first person he could find to send out, not caring much how suitable she was, because he really was in a desperate hurry for Camilla to return home?

It was such a tempting hypothesis that all the caution

in her nature rose to reject it. Instead of answering Matthew's question, she said, "Anyway, it would be nice if Roberta went on liking her, wouldn't it? She just might. She'll enjoy grooming her, if Joanne will let her. She's tried to do it to me all my life and can't forgive me because it's simply beyond her."

"Don't you mean because it isn't necessary? She's got her style, you've got yours. Neither of you will ever be able to correct the other's faults." He got up from his chair and stood smiling down at her. "Good night, my dear."

"Good night, Matthew."

As he left Camilla stretched out in the long wicker chair and gazed up vacantly at the starry sky. She was puzzled at Matthew having shown such strong suspicions of Joanne. It wasn't like him. Usually he was very tolerant in a detached way, even if he did not seem to take warmly to many people.

She was not sure how long she had lain there before Roberta returned. The light on the terrace had not been turned on, so it was just possible, Camilla realised, that Roberta really did not know that she was not alone when she started talking aloud to herself in the sitting-room.

"Camilla's got to go," she said. "I can't stand the way she looks at me any longer. She looks as if she hates me."

A silence followed.

"This girl," Roberta went on, "she may be all right, but in any case I'll put up with her till Camilla's gone. Then, if she won't do, I'll look for someone myself."

There was another silence.

Camilla had sat up, meaning to call out and warn Roberta that she could hear everything that she was saying, but she always felt an awful curiosity on occasions like this to know what Roberta was going to say next. Camilla had not called out when Roberta started again.

"Poor Camilla, she's such a fool, but nothing and nobody has ever been able to stop her doing what she's made up her mind to do, and if she's made up her mind to wreck her life, she'd better get on with it. But what a waste. There's Matthew, hopelessly in love with her. I've never seen him look at anyone as he looks at her, since Moira died. And he's worth a dozen Christopher Peters. And there'd be others if she'd give herself half a chance. Oh well——"

The thudding of Roberta's crutches came towards the door.

Camilla said nothing about having overheard her. She lay back, shut her eyes and acted as if she had dozed off out there in the warm darkness. Roberta remained standing in the doorway for a moment, watching her, then slowly went away again.

Camilla stayed as she was for some minutes.

It was odd, but it had genuinely never occurred to her how very convenient it would be for Roberta if she were to marry Matthew.

It would be more convenient for Camilla if Matthew were to marry Roberta.

But that was hardly likely to happen. For whoever married Roberta would have to be a nurse, rather than a husband. And for all her love of charming other men, it would be a long time before Roberta allowed anyone to compete with her memories of Justin.

CHAPTER IV

HOWEVER, during the days that followed, Roberta put a lot of effort into charming Joanne. She flattered her, joked with her, positively sparkled for her, and even when Joanne was not there, said almost nothing sneering or even condescending about her.

Joanne herself seemed unresponsive, although, in her own fashion, sufficiently content. She did not go out of her way to enthuse about the beauties of Madeira, or the pleasures of continuous sunshine and swimming in the wonderfully warm, clear sea. She seemed to have no curiosity about the mountains, or to want to explore the town, or even to go out much. Camilla introduced her to the Tourist Club and took her to swim there once or twice, but what Joanne seemed really to like to do with her free afternoons was to lie on her bed and read magazines.

She appeared willing enough to learn Roberta's needs, but helped her with a casualness which Camilla was sure could not please Roberta at all. Yet she only winced a little if Joanne pulled her dress off too hastily, and gave Joanne her brilliant smile and loaded her with thanks.

Once, when Joanne and Camilla were at the Tourist Club, they saw Alec Davy, and Camilla knew that he had seen them, for his eyes looked straight into hers with immediate recognition. But then he turned his back and she did not catch him looking at her again. But when Joanne was in the water he swam towards her and they talked for a minute or two.

When Joanne returned from her swim and stretched out in the sun, she remarked, "Now that's a character. Did you see him talking to me? He really is what I call a character. D'you know what he was saying to me? He was saying again if I got into any trouble with you to go to him. God! Can you see it? Can you see anyone going to him if they were in trouble? He hardly knows his own way around, let alone helping anyone else. Anyway, he's found a pretty comfortable place for fighting his sister's battles for her, hasn't he, swimming and lying around in the sun and probably eating his head off? Do you know what his job is?"

"I think Julie told me he was an archaeologist at one of the new universities—I forget which," Camilla answered.

"Is that how he has the time to get away like this, then? I was beginning to wonder a bit if there wasn't something rum about his being able to hang around here."

"Rum?"

"Suspicious, kind of."

"He's only been here a few days," Camilla said.

"Yes, but he said he's going to stay till he's got that

written apology, didn't he, and I don't see Mrs. Ellison —Roberta, I mean—now that I know her a bit, writing it for him. She's a bit of a character too. I shouldn't like to get up against her—though I like her, of course. We're getting along much better than I expected when I first saw her."

"How do you like it here in general?" Camilla asked.

"Oh, I like it a lot. The sun and all. The way I feel at the moment, I could stay for ever."

Camilla began, hesitantly, to think of leaving.

But Joanne had spoken too soon. Later that afternoon she had an attack of the affliction commonly known as "Madeira tummy". That, at least, was what Roberta diagnosed when Joanne appeared at dinner looking green, refused food, and after a few minutes had to rush precipitately out of the room. Roberta gave her Entero Vioform and as Joanne seemed to be abnormally scared by her sudden illness, tried to reassure her by telling her that everyone got it sooner or later and that it would soon pass.

But next day Joanne still looked green and scared and would not come out of her room.

"It isn't mortal," Roberta told her, beginning to grow impatient. "Cheer up. The less you worry about it, the better."

Joanne seemed to make an effort to cheer up and in the afternoon went out for a short walk, but on returning home went back to bed and that evening again touched hardly any food.

It was in the afternoon of the day after that, when Joanne was still in her bedroom and Camilla was drowsing on the terrace, that Roberta came out to her and told her in a hoarse whisper and with her blue eyes wildly staring, that her turquoise and diamond ear-rings had disappeared.

"They've gone, Camilla—out of my jewel-box," she whispered. "Clean gone. I've been hunting for them everywhere, in case I mislaid them, but actually I *know* I didn't. They were in the box. Somebody's taken them."

"No!" Camilla said violently.

"Sh!" Roberta said with a quick glance over her shoulder. "It's true."

"It isn't. And I won't stand for it a second time." Camilla hauled herself up from the chair. "It's too much."

"But it's true. I looked in my jewel-box when I went to lie down after lunch and they aren't there."

"What made you look for them then?"

"I wasn't looking for them. I'd got tired of wearing that aquamarine ring I've had on for the last day or two. My hands have got so thin lately, it's too loose for me, and it always slips round and I get irritated with it. So I took it off and was putting it back in the box when I saw the ear-rings were gone."

Camilla looked at her watch. "You found it out after lunch and it's half past three now. You've taken a long time deciding to come and tell me about it."

Roberta gave another glance over her shoulder. "Don't talk so loud. I told you, I thought perhaps I'd mislaid them, so I hunted everywhere, thinking of all the places I could have put them down when I took them off the last time I wore them. I don't mean I really thought I'd mislaid them. I knew I'd put them back in the box. All the same, one does do crazy things sometimes and have black-outs about them, so I hunted right through all my drawers and pockets and handbags. Then I sat and thought for a time."

"Concocting all this prior to asking me to 'cope' with it for you, just like last time. No. I'm not going to do it. Once was enough. Nobody's going to believe this story."

"But it's true." Roberta grasped Camilla's arm with fingers which, if they were thin, had grown surprisingly strong through handling her crutches. "The other time, well, that was different. I know it was unfair to Julie, but I simply couldn't face your going away so soon. I *had* to do something, can't you understand that? But this time it's absolutely true."

"Just a minute." It was the first time that Roberta had

actually admitted that she had lied about Julie Davy. "You made up that whole story against Julie, you ordered those things yourself, you put them in her drawer and then came and asked me to get rid of her——"

"Yes, yes, yes!" Interrupting impatiently, Roberta lowered herself into a chair. "It was the only thing I could think of. If I'd asked you to stay, if I'd *begged* you, you wouldn't have, would you? And I simply couldn't face being left to strangers yet."

"D'you know, I believe you're the most immoral woman I've ever met," Camilla remarked.

"That's quite untrue," said Roberta. "And the girl bored me. When they're as young as that they always bore me. They've no conversation. And I bored her too, of course, although she was always so bloody sweet about it. At least this woman isn't sweet. She's crude, but she isn't sweet. But that's not the point. The thing is, I'm much better now. I'm much more in control of myself and I wouldn't dream of doing a thing like that again. The ear-rings *have* gone. And I'm not asking you to cope with anything." Her eyes flashed with real anger. "I'm going to ask the police to cope with it."

"One thing at a time, Roberta," Camilla said. "I'm not going to talk about the ear-rings till we've got this matter of Julie cleared up completely. You've just told me you faked the evidence against her to get rid of her. All right, you're going to write a letter to Mr. Davy saying that you're deeply distressed at the unhappiness you caused his sister, that the matter has been completely cleared up since her departure, that the whole thing was a mistake and that you're ready to write her the best of references. Do that now. Then we'll talk about the ear-rings."

Roberta gave a wry smile. "Letting me off lightly, aren't you? It isn't like you. Why don't you insist on my telling the man the whole damn' story, and grovelling to him in the hope he won't sue me?"

"It *is* letting you off lightly," Camilla agreed. "That's because—oh, the reasons you gave for what you did are perfectly true. You weren't fit to be left and I ought to have seen that."

"Dear, sweet Camilla, so kind for once," Roberta said ironically. "Only I'm not going to write that letter."

"You are."

"No, I'm not. Whatever I've done, I will not grovel to anyone."

"I've just given you a formula that lets you off the grovelling."

"The man will know it's grovelling and will want more. And more and more, till he's got enough for a lawsuit and damages. That's what he really came for."

"No, he didn't, and he won't sue you if he gets that apology."

"Of course he will. That's obvious. No, my dear, no letter. Nothing in writing."

"Then I'll write a letter myself and take it to the Vila Angela this afternoon."

"Do what you like, only leave me out of it," Roberta said. "And if he comes here, asking me any questions, I shall absolutely deny this conversation ever took place. That's that. Now about my ear-rings, I've been trying to remember when I saw them last, but I'm not absolutely sure. I think it was a couple of days ago. I keep them in a lower tray and I haven't happened to look at it for some days. So Joanne could have taken them any time to-day or yesterday while she's been pretending to be ill. But they're my favourite pieces of jewellery. It's not just that they're moderately valuable, they were one of the first presents Justin ever gave me, and they were his favourites too. He liked me in them better than in any other jewellery I had. So if that woman's taken them, she isn't going to get away with it."

Camilla sighed. "Roberta, you're hopeless. You *are* hopeless."

Roberta gave her a vague stare that seemed to by-pass her, as if Camilla were no longer a part of her calculations.

"Perhaps I ought to give her a chance before I call the police," she said. "If she isn't a real criminal, but just has some sort of mental quirk, I'd be satisfied if she gave me the ear-rings back."

"And went home?"

"Oh yes, naturally. Of course she'd have to go."

"You haven't mentioned if she broke into your jewel-case," Camilla said. "Did she smash the lock, or did you just happen to leave it open?"

"But I never lock it." Roberta's gaze focused on Camilla's face again and she smiled faintly. "You know the thing—it isn't a jewel-case, it's just a pretty old papier-mâché box. I've always kept my jewellery in it, but I think it's probably a workbox. It hasn't got a lock. And I've never dreamt of keeping any of my things locked up. I don't believe in it. For one thing, Ione's utterly honest and if a thief of some sort broke into the house, he'd make short work of any jewel-case I had, and he'd probably make a good deal of mess as well, smashing things while he hunted around. No, all she had to do was open the box and take what she wanted."

"So she took one of the few things she's seen you wearing, one of the things she'd know for certain you'd miss at once."

"Yes, that's odd, isn't it?" Roberta seemed impressed by this thought. "That's very odd, when you come to think of it. But perhaps that's how the mind of a kleptomaniac works. Perhaps seeing one actually wearing the thing rouses her envy——"

"Roberta!" Camilla said furiously. "Stop it, will you? You're making me sick. I know you can go and find those ear-rings any time you want—and without sending me to search Joanne's room. Now write that letter for me to take to Mr. Davy."

Roberta's face went white with anger. "I've told you, I won't write any letter. You needn't argue. I won't."

"Then I'll go and tell him the truth."

"Go, go! Go anywhere you like! Go home!"

"I think perhaps I'd better, don't you?"

"Yes—go!"

They had both raised their voices. For the moment Camilla had quite forgotten how sounds carried through the little house. It made her start violently when she heard Joanne asking, from just behind her, "Is anything wrong?"

How much of the row she had heard, Camilla did not know. Joanne looked pale, in spite of her new tan, and it seemed to Camilla that the shiny gleam of panic, which she had seen once before in Joanne's eyes, was back in them. Her hair hung untidily round her face. She was in a short, frilly, peach-coloured dressing-gown, and obviously nothing else.

Roberta drew a long breath. Her hands were shaking.

"Just a little argument," she said. "They happen in the best families. What a charming dressing-gown."

"This? Oh, I was just lying down. I'm not feeling too good yet, and it's so hot . . . I'm not sure heat really agrees with me. But as a matter of fact, I was thinking of going for a swim, only I didn't know if you might want me." Looking uncertainly from Roberta to Camilla, Joanne added. "You're sure there's nothing wrong?"

"Absolutely nothing," Roberta answered, twining her fingers together to steady their trembling. "You know, Joanne, that colour's absolutely right for you. It does something for your skin, now that it's beginning to tan a little. And you know your afternoons are absolutely your own. If you want to go and swim, of course you can go."

"All right then. Thanks." Joanne went back through the sitting-room to her bedroom.

When they had heard her door close, Camilla said in a carefully lowered voice, "Still dishing out the flattery."

"Well, I don't see the point of quarrelling till I've decided what to do." Roberta reached for her crutches and with one of them began her quiet little game of lizard chasing. "I think I'll discuss the situation with Matthew first. Then, unless he advises me very strongly against it, I'll call in the police."

"Matthew's already taken a dislike to Joanne," Camilla said.

"And he's very shrewd. But he wouldn't be unfair." Roberta gave a tight-lipped little smile. "Well, aren't you going to see your Mr. Davy?"

"Yes. Only you'll be quite alone here, if Joanne's going out. I can put it off till later."

Once a week Ione had a whole day off to visit her family who lived on the north side of the island, and this happened to be the day.

"No, for God's sake, go. Go and get it over." Roberta jabbed so swiftly at a lizard that she almost touched its flicking tail. "I'm going to lie down. I'm feeling rotten. This new shock . . . But to hell with everything! I'm going to lie down and sleep and presently I'll phone Matthew."

She grasped the arms of her chair, pushed herself up, shifted her weight on to her crutches and moved slowly away to her room.

Going to her own room, Camilla clipped the dark shades on to her glasses, tied a scarf over her hair and, since Joanne had taken the car, started out down the hill on foot.

She had never been to the Vila Angela, but she knew where it was. It was an oldish house not far from the Ponte Monumental. Once it had been a private house and as such must have been quite impressive. It was of the usual cream colour with a red pantile roof, had small balconies with wrought-iron railings at all the windows and a high, blank, cream-coloured wall, topped with a little coping of pantiles, enclosing the garden. An allamanda, covered in blazing yellow bloom, clung to the ironwork of the first floor balconies.

Camilla opened the wooden door in the wall, which led into a small garden, shaded by a tall eucalyptus, which gave a tangy scent to the air. The tough, broad-bladed grass of the small lawn was so neatly trimmed that it looked as if it had been done by hand with a pair of scissors. There were some gaudy clumps of bird-of-paradise flowers in a bed in the middle of the lawn, and a bizarre collection of cacti on each side of a short flight of steps leading up to a door. The door was open. Camilla went up to it and rang.

A page-boy appeared. He looked about eleven years old and had all the dark, supple beauty and cheeky poise of the local children. In English of a sort he told her that Mr. Davy was out but that she was welcome to wait for him, if she wanted, and he showed her to a chair in the garden. Since the boy could not tell her if Mr. Davy would be out for ten minutes, half an hour, an hour or three hours, she was not sure if she wanted to wait, but hoping that perhaps he would come soon she sat down. She was not looking forward to the interview with Alec Davy, did not quite know what she intended to say, had no idea how he would take it, but only knew for certain that she wanted to get it over as quickly as possible.

A celebration of some sort was going on in the town. Every few minutes there was a bang-bang of firecrackers. Camilla had become so used to these since coming to Madeira that she hardly noticed them, but the noise grievously annoyed an elderly German couple, the only other people in the garden, who were quietly and fiercely enjoying a good quarrel of the kind that the long-married go in for on holidays, and they did not want to be distracted.

Camilla's German was not quite up to telling her what the quarrel was about, except that it was something to do with their digestions. It seemed that something that they had eaten had upset them both and they could not agree on what it had been. Soon their hectoring voices began to get on her nerves as much as the firecrackers did on theirs. She started to get up to go. But at once she felt convinced that if she waited only a few minutes more Alec Davy would come in. Sitting down again, she let some minutes pass. Then she repeated the manœuvre, starting to get up, changing her mind and sitting down. She had done this about three times when the page-boy reappeared, bringing her an English newspaper to read.

She read that there was a financial crisis in Britain, that

the usual wars were continuing in the Far East, that three men had escaped from Dartmoor, were armed and considered dangerous, that two Cabinet Ministers had swapped jobs without any noticeable signs of rejoicing from anybody, that a stately home had been broken into and jewellery worth seventy-five thousand pounds stolen, that some pop singer had married a female judo expert, that a bank had been robbed.

The things that happen, she thought. What did it really feel like to be involved in any of the newsworthy events mentioned? Here was she, growing more and more distraught merely at the thought of having to admit to a fairly harmless-seeming man a little frame-up, almost the littlest frame-up possible, which had done no serious harm to anybody apart from leaving a scar on a girl's memory. A nasty scar, of course. All scars are nasty. All the same, what had gone on in the minds of those Cabinet Ministers, of the men who had stolen those jewels, or robbed the bank? What hopes, what thrills, what disappointments, what black fears? She was pondering this when Alec Davy came in through the gate in the wall.

He looked as if he had been for a long walk. His shoes were coated with dust, his shirt and shorts clung to him stickily and he had an air of comfortable tiredness. He wore a straw hat on the back of his head and for a moment the sight of him carried Camilla back to the afternoon in Roberta's house, when Julie had come in gaily and innocently from her swim, twirling on her finger the immense straw hat that she had just bought. But then he saw Camilla and his look changed as completely as Julie's had when she had understood why Camilla wanted to speak to her.

His look did not change in the way for which she had been prepared. It did not become angry or scornful or suspicious, but only startled, worried, and rather scared. In fact, he looked inclined to turn tail and disappear immediately through the door in the wall. Camilla guessed that to be successfully angry, he needed time and perhaps drink to stoke the flames. Taken by surprise, his instinct was to be, at the least, courteous.

"Good evening," he said.

She stood up and said, "Good evening."

He remained about two yards away, and began turning his hat round in his hands.

"Did you come to see me?" he asked.

"Yes," she said.

"You wanted to talk?"

"Yes."

"Have we anything to talk about?"

"Yes, but perhaps not here." She was aware that the German couple had suddenly grown silent, the question of whether it had been the mayonnaise or the green figs that had upset their stomachs left temporarily unsettled.

He glanced at the couple, nodded and said, "No, of course not. Where shall we go?"

"Perhaps for a short walk."

He nodded again. "Would you mind waiting a minute or two while I go and clean up a little?"

"I'm in no hurry."

"Then I'll just go . . ." He paused. "There is some point in this, is there? I don't enjoy argument for its own sake, and you know where I stand."

"There's a lot of point in it," she said. "I want to talk to you very badly."

He almost smiled then, as if her tone told him why she had come.

"We could walk out along the mole," he said. "There are several ships in. Do you enjoy looking at ships?"

"Sometimes, but I'm not expecting to enjoy our talk. I've come to grovel, if you want to know the general line I'm going to take."

"Oh God, don't do that—I've never wanted you to do that," he said unhappily. "Just something in writing —a line or two—to take back to Julie. I've calmed down a lot since I got here. It's the climate, perhaps. It's just too difficult to go on being angry in all this sunshine.

And I expect Julie did behave hysterically. She's a terribly emotional creature."

"No, no, she did the only thing she could have," Camilla said. "But I'd like to explain, if I can, how it really happened. Then perhaps you won't feel you ought to be quite as angry with us as you were. I don't mean I want to excuse it, but I've a feeling that if you understood how —why—well, that in a sense it was all my fault, but that I honestly didn't grasp that in time—well, you might not hate us too much, and you can go away without worrying any more about us."

"I'm not sure I want to go away," he said. "I like it here. If I could get this affair of Julie off my mind, I'd settle down to a perfect holiday. I've just had a day up in the mountains, walking. You know it all, I expect—that place where almost nothing grows but that giant heather —but to me it's marvellous. I'm almost thankful Julie put it into my head to come. The change from what it's like down here at sea-level to the pines and those extraordinary bare peaks . . . But I'm keeping you. I'll just clean up, then we can go and look at the ships."

Smiling really warmly now, he turned and went into the house.

In about a minute he was out again. He was not alone. He had Joanne Willis with him and was gripping her above the elbow. The anger that he had not been able to summon up when he met Camilla made his brown face a dull brick red. He pulled Joanne down the steps from the doorway so violently that she almost fell. Swinging her round so that she and Camilla faced one another, he asked Camilla furiously, "What's this you've cooked up together? Why was this woman searching my room?"

"I wasn't searching your room!" Joanne cried. "I wasn't, I was waiting for you. You told me, if I was in trouble, to come to you. I'm in trouble and I came!"

"How did you get in?" he asked.

"I tipped that kid to take me up," she said. "I'd have waited in the garden, but I saw Miss Carey waiting there—she was reading a paper, which is why she didn't see me—so I gave the kid a few escudos to take me to your room. I told him to tell you I was there when you got in. He forgot, or perhaps he didn't understand. But you did say, if I was in trouble to come to you."

Looking as if he rather wished he hadn't, Alec Davy let her go. He clawed at his red-brown hair. "That's right, I did." He turned back to Camilla. "Didn't you sit down here, waiting to catch me and take me out for that little walk while she went through my things?"

"I wasn't going through your things!" Joanne cried. "I was just waiting."

"Then why were all the drawers open? Why was my suitcase open? Why were all my things on the floor?"

"How should I know?" she said. "They were like that when I went in. I thought you were just an untidy type."

"I'm not. I'm very tidy. I can't bear untidiness."

"How was I to know that?"

"All the same, you seemed to be counting my handkerchiefs."

"I wasn't, I was just wandering about, thinking about how I was going to tell you what happened."

"What *has* happened?"

Camilla was acutely conscious of the silence of the German couple, whose intestinal anxieties had had a miraculous cure. Only the banging of the firecrackers continued.

"Mightn't we in any case go for that little walk?" she said.

"I don't want to walk anywhere," said Joanne. "I just want to have a talk with Mr. Davy."

"Then suppose we go for a short drive," Camilla suggested. "You've got the car, haven't you?"

"No, I want to talk to Mr. Davy *alone*!"

"Well?" Camilla said to him.

He thought it over.

"Suppose we do just stroll down to the harbour," he said. "Or anywhere else you like. I've a feeling you've both really come about the same thing, so why shouldn't we talk it over together?"

"I don't think we've come about the same thing," Joanne said. In her smooth, plump face her light brown eyes looked enormous. One cheek was twitching. "I've come because Mrs. Ellison says I've stolen her ear-rings. I heard her saying so to Miss Carey. She's trying to do the same to me as she did to your sister. Only it's a much more serious charge, and she talked about going to the police. She's going to get me put in prison or deported, that's what she's going to do. And so I thought of coming to you, because I thought you might stick up for me. But if you don't want to, well, you won't be the first person who's let me down. I won't be the first who's been let down either. It's just life, that's what it is. But somehow I thought you were different and I could count on you."

The colour of Alec Davy's face had returned to normal, but he frowned formidably.

"Miss Carey, did you come to talk about all this?" he asked.

"Yes and no." Camilla gave up worrying about how much the German couple overheard. But she wished she knew what Joanne had really been doing in his room. Had she been searching it? Could she have had some cock-eyed idea that he had stolen Roberta's ear-rings? It didn't seem possible. But if Joanne had not been searching, who had and why? "I don't think I've arrived at the right time for the talk I had in mind," she said. "Perhaps we could meet to-morrow, Mr. Davy, after you and Miss Willis have had the talk she wants."

"It sounds to me," he said, "as if the talk I want is with Mrs. Ellison."

"All right," Camilla said. "Come up to the house now and let's have everything out into the open."

"If you don't mind . . ." Joanne began hurriedly. Her cheek-muscle was still twitching and she looked as if she did not welcome Camilla's suggestion at all. But then she gave a shrug of her shoulders. "Okay. Why not?"

"Then let's go." Camilla led the way out through the door in the wall to the car that was parked just outside.

They drove up the hill to Roberta's house in silence. Joanne looked sullen and scared, Alec Davy wary and thoughtful, Camilla, as she felt, frustrated and puzzled. Stopping the car at the door, she got out quickly and went in ahead of the others to warn Roberta what to expect.

Because she did this she was the first to see what was on the floor of the sitting-room.

At first, through the doorway, she saw only feet, splayed apart on the waxed boards. Staring at them incredulously, making no sense of them, not wanting to make sense of them, she probably would have stood still if she had not been moving as fast as she was. But her own impetus carried her on into the room, and she saw the rest.

She saw the body of a man there, a man whom she had never seen before. He was not a big man, yet his spread-eagled body seemed to her to cover the whole floor. He was in a brilliantly patterned shirt and freshly pressed cotton trousers. Odd that at such a moment she should have noticed the trousers and how sharp their creases were. He was lying on his face, what was left of it, which was not much, for a good deal of his head had been blasted away. There was an unspeakable mess of blood, brains and bone on the floor, while scattered around him lay a curious collection of objects, one or two ornamental baskets, a bottle of Madeira and several small parcels. In fact, but for the fact that he was dead, murdered, and lying on the floor in the middle of Roberta's sitting-room, he looked like a typical tourist off one of the cruise-ships. His outflung hands looked as if they had reached out as he fell to save his precious souvenirs of his day's visit to Funchal.

Almost beside Camilla a man's voice said quietly, "I was just wondering where everyone had got to."

She started and opened her mouth to scream.

A hand came out and covered it. It was a quite gentle hand, but it was firm and it belonged to Christopher Peters who had been standing flattened against the wall behind the door.

"Quiet, now," he said. "For God's sake, no hysterics, Cam."

CHAPTER V

FOR A MOMENT she did not even think about how strange it was that he should be there, looking as unrumpled, as alert, as handsome in his unobtrusive, well-bred way, as he always did. But at the back of her mind she did think that quite possibly she would never forgive him for telling her not to have hysterics. He had never seen her having hysterics. She was not having them now. What harm, in certain circumstances, does a good healthy scream do? What is there wrong with two or three good screams? They are a perfectly normal reaction to horror, and certainly should not be called hysterics.

Pulling away from him without answering, Camilla pushed past Joanne and Alec Davy in the doorway and burst into Roberta's room.

She was sitting on the edge of her bed, holding her head in both hands and blinking groggily. There were still two beds in the room. They had identical white candlewick bedspreads, but one bed had the geometrically neat look of one without sheets or blankets and that is never used. Roberta often said that she must have it taken away, but she could not make up her mind to do it. The Venetian blinds at the windows were down and the light was dim.

"What's happened?" she asked. "I heard something . . . Somebody . . ."

"Are you all right?" Camilla asked.

"Yes, I suppose so . . . I was asleep. What is it?"

"You said you heard something. What? A scream? A shot?"

"I don't know. I was asleep. Half asleep. Those damned firecrackers—they went on and on. I couldn't get to sleep properly. Then I heard something different."

"How long ago?"

"I don't know. I thought I was dreaming. Perhaps I was. I don't feel very well. I can't stop worrying about those ear-rings disappearing. I've never in my life had to deal with anything like it. I've been lucky. I've always been surrounded by honest people. Now everyone seems to have turned horrible. I don't know what to do."

"Roberta," Camilla said, "this is worse than the ear-rings. There's a man in the sitting-room—dead. In the sitting-room, on the floor. I think he's been shot."

"*Dead?*" Roberta whispered at her.

"Definitely dead."

"Who?"

"I've never seen him before. We'll have to call the police. But I think, if you can manage it, it might be useful, before we do, if you'd come through and tell us who it is."

"Dead!" Roberta repeated. "Camilla, it isn't—you aren't trying to keep it from me—it isn't Matthew?"

"Matthew? Why should it be Matthew?"

"I don't know. It's just that I seem to lose everyone—everything."

"I told you, I've never seen him before," Camilla said.

"Matthew isn't here now?"

"No."

"I telephoned him," Roberta said. "I asked him to come round, and he said he would presently. But then I went to sleep and I can't think of anyone else who would simply come into the house."

"Do you think you can face coming out and taking a look at this man anyway?" Camilla asked.

"Yes, of course." All at once Roberta sounded amazingly collected, as she always was in any serious crisis. It was only the small strains of life that tended to be too much for her. Camilla gave her an arm to hold on to, to help her up to her feet, then handed her her crutches and Roberta made her way to the door.

"There's a man's voice now," she said. "Matthew must just have come."

"No, it isn't Matthew, but I'll phone him to come round at once, or I'll go and fetch him." Camilla opened the door for her: "He'll be able to help with the police. Now let me warn you, this isn't going to be nice . . ."

Roberta clicked her tongue irritably, as if this were a waste of words, and hobbled on into the sitting-room.

Christopher had emerged from behind the door. Standing in the doorway that led out to the terrace, he was drawing deep breaths, as if he found it difficult to get enough air. He was more shaken than Camilla had realised in her first glimpse of him. Alec Davy was on the terrace, leaning against the wrought-iron railing, looking as if he might be sick over it. Only Joanne was in the room. She was standing near the splayed feet of the dead man with a strange sparkle in her light brown eyes and what incredibly seemed to be a smile on her lips.

Camilla found it far harder to look at him a second time than when she had first blundered into the room. Keeping her eyes down so that all that she saw of him were his feet and those wonderfully pressed trousers, she waited for Roberta to speak.

She did so crisply. "I've never seen him in my life." Then she looked at Christopher. "I haven't seen you either. Who are you?"

"My name's Christopher Peters," he answered.

"Oh," she said, "*that* man."

"Yes—I'm sorry, that man."

"And what are you doing here?"

"I came to fetch Cam home."

"Indeed. She asked you to do so, did she?"

"No, that's why I came," he said.

She gestured at the floor. "Do you know who this man is?"

"No."

"Does any of you?"

No one answered till, after a moment, Joanne said, "No."
It took Alec Davy a little longer to echo it. "No."

"I don't believe it," Roberta said. "Someone here knows
him, or why should he have come here at all?"

"To burgle the place, perhaps," Christopher suggested.
"You seem to leave all your doors wide open. That's how I
got in just now and found him."

Roberta made the same irritable clicking sound with her
tongue as before. It sounded as it might have if she were
annoyed with someone for having spilled wine on the
carpet or let a cigarette-end burn a hole in a chair-cover.

"Would you set out to burgle a place with your arms
filled with baskets and bottles of Madeira?" she demanded.

"Protective colouring, perhaps," he said.

"Absurd. I believe you and he came here together. You
certainly know who he is."

"We did not come here together and I don't know who he
is." Christopher had stopped gasping for air and was at
his very calmest. There was never anything like an attack on
him to bring the steely quality in him to the surface.

Perhaps Roberta recognised this for she turned on
Joanne. "Then he came to see you."

Joanne only gave a shake of her head. But the sparkle
was still in her eyes, her face was lit up with excitement and
the animation made it almost beautiful. She appeared to
find murder a very exhilarating change in a humdrum
life.

"Mr. Davy?" said Roberta.

"Well, I've been thinking," he said. "I believe I've seen
him."

"You said you hadn't."

"I said I didn't know him. I don't. But I've seen him. I
couldn't be wrong about that shirt. I was down by the
harbour this morning before I went off walking and I saw
him come off the cruise-ship that docked last night."

"That's mad," Roberta said. "Everything's mad or

else I am. A man gets off a cruise-ship, buys a lot of souvenirs, comes up to the home of a woman he's never met before, and gets himself murdered in her sitting-room. Isn't that mad—too mad to be true?"

"You're perfectly right, of course," Christopher said.

"So at least someone here is lying."

"And it might even be you, Mrs. Ellison," he said.

She blinked rapidly in slight shock at his swift answer, then gave him a hard stare and said, "I'm afraid you and I are not going to like one another."

"Now oughtn't we to be calling the police?" he said. "I'd offer to do it for you, but I don't speak Portuguese."

She turned to Camilla. "Call Matthew, will you? He's the person we need here."

Camilla heartily agreed with her and went to the telephone.

It had not struck her as strange that Christopher had hardly looked at her since she had come back into the room, or spoken directly to her. She was so accustomed to the fact that nowadays, when there were other people present, he and she ignored one another, that she would have been astonished if he had done anything else.

What had struck her as very strange was that he should have stated without any reserve that he had come to fetch her home. Of course, he had had to give Roberta some explanation for being here in her house. All the same, it was strange, it was unlike him. He was seldom caught off balance. There was deliberation behind most of what he did. If it had not been for that mysterious and dreadful dead man, with his absurd baskets and bottles, in the sitting-room, Camilla would certainly have given more thought than she did to this uncharacteristic action of Christopher's. As it was, a troubled awareness of it only flashed through her mind and was gone again.

Matthew arrived in about two minutes. He telephoned the police station, stopped Roberta covering the body, as she wanted to, herded everyone out on to the terrace, brought out drinks for them and handed them round.

There was something very steadying in his presence. Here was a man who was not stunned by the ghastly novelty of looking at a murdered man. There was no risk that he might be sick over the terrace railing. However, he barely spoke and asked no questions and it was in a rather grisly silence that they waited for the police to arrive.

When they did, Matthew went out to meet them. There were three of them, two *Agente da Policia*, both in grey cotton uniforms, with truncheons hanging from their broad leather belts, the third a *Chefe da Policia Judiciaria*, whose name was Raposo, a shortish, slender, very good-looking man, with smooth dark hair, big melancholy eyes and a thin, fine-boned face. He wore a lightweight fawn suit, a snowy shirt and shoes with thick rubber soles on which he moved quite silently.

Later more police arrived and took photographs and sprayed grey powder everywhere. They inked the fingers of everyone there and took their fingerprints. A doctor came and examined the body and said that the man had been dead for not more than two hours or less than one. Someone drew an outline of the body with chalk on Roberta's floor, the body was removed on a stretcher to a mortuary somewhere, then photographs were taken of the chalk drawing on the floor.

Camilla had no idea how many hours passed while this went on. All the time the *Chefe da Policia Judiciaria* asked questions. One after the other, he had everyone into the dining-room, where he had established himself with another plain-clothes officer, who took notes, and with Matthew, who was there to help in case of language difficulties, and asked questions. Questions and questions.

The Chefe was a soft-voiced, very dignified, very thorough man, so thorough, so careful, so intent on being certain that he had understood the precise meaning of what was said to him, that after a little while the person whom he was interrogating wanted to lose his head and his manners and start shouting at the quiet little man. Which, no doubt, was just what the Chefe was hoping for.

First on his list was Roberta. When she went into the dining-room and the door closed behind her, Camilla found herself alone on the terrace with Alec Davy.

He said, "Do you realise, Miss Carey, I still don't know why you came to see me this afternoon?"

Joanne and Christopher were walking together round the little garden below, talking in low voices. They were going from clump to clump of exotic flowers and except that it appeared an unlikely subject for conversation at such a time, it might have been thought that Joanne was telling Christopher what flowers they were. Something about their confidential air was disconcerting to Camilla. It looked as if they were better acquainted than she had realised.

Watching them uneasily, she replied, "No, I never got round to telling you, did I? I'd forgotten about it."

She turned her head to look at Alec Davy. His curly red-brown hair clung damply to his forehead. In his sticky shirt and dusty shoes, which he had never had the chance to change, he still looked as if he had just come in from a long walk, but instead of looking comfortably relaxed, he looked tense and nervous.

"You said you wanted to talk to me very badly," he said. "We were going to walk down to the harbour. I told you I'd like to look at the ships. I like to watch them loading the casks of Madeira on to them. Have you ever watched that?"

"No, as a matter of fact, I haven't," she said.

"They're beautiful—the casks. Oak, I think, and perfectly beautifully made. And they're going off all over the world. I find that extraordinarily exciting. If I hadn't somehow got into archaeology I think I'd have liked a job as a harbour master. Why *did* you want to talk to me so badly, Miss Carey?"

"It was about Julie."

"I supposed so."

"It seems insignificant now."

"Perhaps it isn't."

"No, I know it isn't. It's only that I'm having some

difficulty concentrating. I can't remember exactly what I meant to say." She leant her hot forehead on her hands. "Tell me, this morning, when you were down on the mole, were you watching the ships for this man who came here?"

"No, I wasn't. I've an absolutely disinterested love of harbours. About Julie . . ."

"Yes." Camilla leant back in her chair. "I came to see you to tell you I knew she hadn't ordered those things from Godhino's. I was going to tell you I'd got my sister to admit she put the things there herself. I was going to offer to write a letter of apology to Julie. And I was going to ask you to let my sister off as lightly as you could, because she's a very sick woman, and what happened to Julie is my fault, because I didn't really face how ill she was."

"I don't think I understand," he said, wrinkling his forehead.

"Roberta wanted me to stay on, you see," Camilla said. "You know, don't you, that Justin, her husband, died suddenly about six weeks ago? And she'd depended on him for everything ever since her accident four years ago. It wasn't just for the physical help she needs, it was for everything. Company, talk, friendship—for his friends too. He was one of the most lovable people I've ever known. He had dozens of friends. And he surrounded Roberta with them, and she managed to stay wonderfully cheerful—you'd have been astonished—although she knew she was never going to walk properly again. But now somehow most of these people seem to have melted away. They were his friends, you see, not hers. When he died they all came here with condolences, and they still drop in now and then because they feel they ought to, but she's really awfully lonely."

"She's a difficult woman, perhaps," Alec Davy suggested.

"Oh yes, she's difficult."

"So it's her own fault."

"Of *course* it's her own fault, except that it wasn't her fault being turned into a cripple, when she was used to being successful with everyone simply by being such a beauty that she'd never had to learn how to make them *like* her. Don't you see, that left her utterly helpless when Justin died? And she needed me with her then because I wasn't a stranger. And if I'd accepted that and promised to stay with her until she was used to Julie, and perhaps grown very fond of her, none of that horrible business would have happened."

"But haven't you a life of your own to live?" he asked.

"Of a sort, yes." She looked sombrely down at the garden.

Christopher and Joanne were no longer talking to one another down there. They had drawn a little apart, with Christopher moving on ahead, looking thoughtfully at the flower-beds, but obviously not really seeing them, while Joanne watched him, as if she wanted to go on talking to him, but had realised that he no longer wanted to talk to her.

After a short pause, Alec Davy said, "What about the ear-rings? Has your sister played the same trick a second time, or has that girl really taken them?"

"I don't know. But it doesn't strike me as likely, somehow, that Joanne took them," Camilla answered.

"So you think your sister's at it again."

"I suppose so. But at least I've realised now how serious the situation is and that she *can't* be left to herself yet."

"That girl *was* searching my room, you know," he said. "It had been turned upside down and she'd got a hand right inside the drawer where I've got my handkerchiefs and ties and so on. She jumped right away from it as soon as she heard me, but she was too late. I saw her."

"Do you mean she was looking for the ear-rings there? Surely that doesn't make sense."

"No, but perhaps she'd had the bloody silly idea there was something there that might be worth stealing. Perhaps she really is a thief. Ironic for your sister, in the circumstances, if it's so."

"Then again, perhaps Joanne told you the truth," Camilla said, "and she really did find the room upside down because someone else had already done the searching. And when she saw it like that, she couldn't resist poking around a little."

He looked sceptical. "A sneak-thief is one thing, but do I look the type who travels around with anything worth actually searching for, like valuables or secret papers?"

"No, but they never do look it, do they?—the people who really do it."

"I swear I've never sold a secret about prehistoric man to any Russian agent yet," he said. "But I suppose I don't look much the type to get mixed up in a murder either. Yet here I am. And so are you."

She lifted her hands and let them drop again, palms turned emptily upwards.

"And none of us even knows who the man is," she said. "All the same, he must have come here for a reason . . ."

She was interrupted by Christopher who came suddenly and swiftly up the terrace steps. The way that he did it, and the way that he stood over them, made it seem as if he were deliberately breaking in on them, having found something that he did not like about their quiet way of talking.

"Has it struck you that the man could have come here *without* any reason?" he asked them. "He could simply have come to the wrong address, and been followed here and shot because it was as good a place for a murder as any?"

"Yes, I'd thought of that," said Alec Davy.

"I think he came to see Joanne," Camilla said.

She felt fairly sure that that was what Christopher and Joanne had been talking about down there in the garden. Joanne had been confiding in Christopher, asking him for help and advice. A lot of people turned to him for help and advice. It seemed to come naturally. He struck them as both sympathetic and bold, as practical and imaginative, as capable of decisive action yet tolerant of their fears of it. A perfect counsellor.

"Didn't you see her face when she saw him?" she went

on. "She knew him and it seemed to me she was jolly glad that he was dead."

Christopher shook his head at her slightly. "I'd watch what you say, Cam. That sort of talk's dangerous."

"Well, perhaps it's just that she's got a liking for murder." She looked up at him as he stood leaning against the terrace railing. "Where are you staying for the night?"

"At Reid's, of course."

Of course. For Christopher always the best. She need hardly have inquired.

"Are you sure you can get a room there?"

"I've got one," he said. "I cabled before I left."

They were speaking in the casual tones that they always used in front of other people and suddenly this became one of the things that was happening on that horrible evening that were unbearable. Camilla started to get up. She was not sure what she meant to do, go down into the garden and walk round and round it at a furious pace, or plunge through the police-filled sitting-room to her own room. But just then an agente came out on to the terrace and asked Christopher to accompany him to the dining-room for a talk with the Senhor Chefe.

As Christopher went indoors, Alec Davy's eyes followed him with a thoughtful, perceptive look on his odd, lumpy-featured face. A disturbing face, a troll's face, not quite human, it occurred to Camilla suddenly. Julie's face also had had something not quite human about it, an elfin quality. But her brother's was more the kind that should belong to one of those strange Norse creatures who live in caverns, inside dark mountains.

"Now there's a man," he said, "who really might have valuables or secrets worth searching for in his room. A formidable man."

"But it was your room they searched," Camilla said.

"They? She. It was that woman."

"Well, you'll tell the police about it, I suppose. But I wonder . . . If you could manage not to mention those ear-rings . . ."

"I can see that might make things easier for your sister," he said.

"They can't have anything to do with this man's murder, can they?"

"It does seem unlikely."

"And it would be kind."

"As my uncle, the bishop, told me I always should be. I'm sorry about the bishop, Miss Carey. Julie faked that reference somehow, the little idiot. And let me come out here without warning me about it. There'll be some strong words spoken when I get home. But I owe you something on account of it. I'll say nothing about the ear-rings, if I can help it."

But it was Camilla the Chefe wanted to interrogate next, when he had finished with Christopher.

To begin with the melancholy-eyed Chefe treated her rather as if he were a doctor whose sad duty it was to inform her that she was suffering from a mortal disease, and who was trying to put off the unpleasant moment when he must do it for as long as possible. He asked her how she liked Madeira. Did she like the food, the wine? Had she made any agreeable excursions into the mountains?

In one corner of the room sat the other detective with his notebook. In another corner sat Matthew, smoking. To judge by the number of stubs in the ashtray beside him, he had been smoking far harder than he usually did, yet he looked relaxed enough, and in some odd way neutral, almost unconcerned with what was going on. Perhaps he felt that he had been asked to sit in on the interviews merely as a courtesy and so meant to be careful not to interfere in any way. Certainly the Chefe had no need of help with the English language. If his accent was not impeccable, his vocabulary was extensive.

"The climate suits you?" he inquired of Camilla with that sad sound of postponing the evil moment of getting down to business. That, at least, was what she thought until she began to realise that he was moving in on the main subject in his own fashion, obliquely.

85

She answered, "Yes, it's wonderful."

"Not too hot for you?"

"Oh no."

"You have been here before, I believe."

"Two or three times, yes, to stay with my sister."

"And now perhaps you will stay on."

She raised her eyebrows inquiringly.

He explained, "I mean, now that Mr. Ellison—who, may I say, was my valued friend, we sometimes played golf together—now that he is dead and your sister is alone, perhaps you will stay on here with us."

"No, I'm planning to go home fairly soon," she said.

"Yet will it not be very sad for Mrs. Ellison to live all alone?"

"Oh, I'll stay for as long as I'm needed," Camilla said. "But it may not be long. Miss Willis is here to take over from me. Or if she doesn't want to stay, or isn't suitable, we'll look for someone else."

"But this can never be the same as having a sister, a member of her own family, living with her," he protested.

She smiled slightly. "Sometimes it can be a great deal better. One's relations aren't always one's best friends."

The detective looked mildly distressed, even shocked. No doubt a man of strong family feelings himself, the attitude common among the Anglo-Saxons that relatives are people whom it is best to keep at a safe distance, that this tends towards the avoidance of strife and helps towards peace of mind, probably struck him as unseemly and unnatural.

"But it is true, isn't it," he said, "that it would be very difficult for Mrs. Ellison if she were quite alone?"

"*Quite* alone?" Camilla said. "Oh yes, she'd be practically helpless."

"Yet she was left quite alone this afternoon."

So that was the point towards which he had been gently sliding.

"Yes," she replied. "The maid, Ione, had the whole day off to visit her family. Miss Willis had gone swimming. And I went out for a bit too."

"Is it usual then for Mrs. Ellison to be left completely alone, even though she is so helpless?" he asked.

"Oh yes. She doesn't mind it for a time. She can move about the house quite well. You've seen it."

"But can she drive a car, or get in and out of it alone?"

"No."

"I see. So without a companion who could drive she could never get out at all and she would be very lonely."

"Yes."

He tapped his beautifully even white teeth with the ballpoint pencil with which he had been doodling on the pad on the table before him. "Now when you went out, 'for a bit', as you say, Miss Carey, where did you go?"

"I went to see Mr. Davy at the Vila Angela."

"He is a friend of yours? You know him well?"

"No, very little."

"Then why did you visit him?"

"To ask him about his sister—how she was getting on and so on." She noticed that Matthew was looking at her with a peculiarly penetrating stare, but his expression told her nothing except that he was interested in the fact that she had been to visit Alec Davy. Odd, she thought, she had never really taken in before what it had meant to Matthew to be a policeman. His loyalties at the moment appeared to be not to his friends but all to this dark little man who was leading her along so gently. "Miss Davy was here for a time before Miss Willis," she went on, "but it didn't work out and she went home."

"She went home very suddenly, didn't she? There was perhaps a quarrel."

"There was a—well, a misunderstanding."

"And is that why Mr. Davy came here—to clear up this misunderstanding?"

"Yes."

"And was that his only reason for coming?"

"Yes, so far as I know."

"You do not think perhaps he had some other reason as well?"

She was puzzled. "Not that I know of. I haven't thought about it. Perhaps you should ask him himself. I went to see him to ask how his sister was and to say how sorry I was that she and my sister hadn't got on better together, and that was all."

This was so near, literally speaking, to the truth, that Camilla was rather pleased. She began almost to enjoy the feeling of walking on eggshells. At the same time she began to wonder if by any chance it could be true that Alec Davy had had some reason other than that of wanting to clear the character of his sister for coming to Madeira. A reason which would explain why his room had been searched, and which would somehow connect him with the mystifying murdered man, and perhaps with Joanne Willis too . . .

"At what time did you arrive at the Vila Angela, Miss Carey?" the Chefe asked.

"At what time?" she said. "I'm not sure. I don't know. It was—oh, I should think it was about four o'clock or a little after. But I wasn't thinking about the time."

"Did you find Mr. Davy there?"

"No, I had to wait quite a long time for him. He was out for a walk, I believe."

"Do you know what time it was when he returned?"

"No. I waited in the garden perhaps half an hour. Something like that. Perhaps the page-boy at the Vila Angela would be able to tell you more exactly. He took me out to the garden and brought me a paper to read. And there was a German couple in the garden. They may have remembered me."

"If this is so, then you have an alibi for the probable time of the murder, but perhaps Mr. Davy has not. When he returned to the pension did you come here immediately?"

"Well, we talked for a little while, then we came here."

"But when you arrived here, I understand Miss Willis was with you."

"Yes."

"How had that come about?"

"Well, she had the car . . ."

At that point Camilla met Matthew's eyes and for the first time since she had come into the room they had some expression in them. Was it warning? She paused uneasily.

The detective said, "Well, she had the car."

"And she came to the Vila Angela," Camilla said.

"Also to see Mr. Davy?"

"Yes."

"They are acquainted, then."

"They travelled out here from Lisbon together. They've said nothing about ever having met before that."

"How soon after you arrived at the Vila Angela did Miss Willis arrive?"

"I don't know."

"But if you were in the garden . . ."

"I didn't notice her come in. I was reading a newspaper."

"But within a few minutes of Mr. Davy arriving, you all drove up here together."

"It was more than a few minutes later. Perhaps a quarter of an hour."

"And you came in ahead of the others and you found the dead man."

"Yes."

"And Mr. Peters."

"Yes."

"Did that surprise you?"

"The dead man or Mr. Peters?"

The Chefe gave the faintest of sad smiles. "Both, Miss Carey. But let us take them one at a time. The dead man, then. I believe you have said that you have never seen him before."

"No, never."

"Are you sure? Did you look at him carefully?"

"No . . . No, not at all carefully." She could not control the shudder that shook her suddenly. "I took one look, then I was careful not to look again. It was so

89

horrible and so fantastic. That utter stranger, with his silly souvenirs, lying there with half his head blown off in the middle of my sister's sitting-room—it didn't seem real, it didn't seem possible. I simply didn't believe in it. I don't quite believe in it now." Her voice was rising and beginning to get out of control. Another look from Matthew steadied her. "I think he must have come here by mistake," she said. "Come to the wrong address, looking for someone who doesn't live here. I don't believe his murder has anything to do with any of us. I know I'd never seen him before."

The Chefe tapped his teeth again with his ballpoint.

"It has been suggested to me by Mr. Peters that he came here by mistake. Concerning Mr. Peters now—he was in the room with the dead man when you entered."

"Yes."

"Were you surprised to see him?"

"In those circumstances, very."

He gave an impatient little frown. "Surprised to see him here in Funchal, Miss Carey? Surprised to see him here at all?"

"Yes, though he mentioned on the telephone some days ago that he might come."

"So, he did?" For once the detective looked a little surprised himself. "Mrs. Ellison seems not to have expected him. She seems to think it very strange that he should have come. She seems convinced that he and the dead man were acquainted."

"Perhaps I didn't tell her that he might be coming," Camilla replied. "I suppose I didn't really think it very likely."

His dark eyes searched her face for a moment.

"Now suppose Mr. Peters is right," he said. "Suppose the dead man came here by mistake, to the wrong address. Suppose he found the door open and came in . . ." He paused and suddenly turned to Matthew. "Mr. Frensham, I know you say it is impossible, but I am going to make the same suggestion to Miss Carey as

I made to you. Miss Carey—suppose Mrs. Ellison, who was lying down in her room, I have been told, and quite alone and helpless in the house, heard a stranger come into it, heard him moving about, behaving suspiciously, suppose she was frightened, as would be natural, and when she went to see who it was, took a gun with her——"

"No, no—impossible! I told you, she hasn't got a gun," Matthew broke in.

"Miss Carey?"

"I'm quite sure she hasn't got a gun," Camilla said.

"But how do you know?"

The truth was, of course, that Camilla did not know. It is very difficult to know what a person has not got. It is much easier to know, at least within limits, what she has got. Has she a house? Yes. Has she a car? Yes. Has she a pair of turquoise and diamond ear-rings? Yes. . . .

But how could Camilla know for sure that hidden among Roberta's old hats, or behind some books, or under a moveable floorboard, she had not kept a gun hidden?

CHAPTER VI

"I'M SURE, that's all," Camilla said.

"You understand that in such circumstances as I have described," the detective said, "no very serious blame could attach to Mrs. Ellison."

"I know—I suppose the charge wouldn't be murder. But I'm sure she hasn't got a gun and didn't do it."

"Yet is there not something strange about the way she claims she heard nothing, or perhaps something, but she does not know what? Is that not strange?"

Camilla herself thought that it was decidedly strange, but she was not going to admit it.

"I don't think so," she said. "She was asleep. Those firecrackers were popping all the afternoon. She was wakened by something that sounded rather like one. When I went into her room, she was sitting there on the edge of her bed, confused, feeling that what had wakened her hadn't really been a firecracker. But of course she didn't guess what it was. She was holding her head, feeling that something was wrong, and she was scared to go out, I think, but that's all. I didn't find it strange."

"Yet the doctor is sure that when he examined the body, the man had been dead for at least an hour. So allowing for the time that it took for you to call the police, and for them and the doctor to arrive, it appears that the man was shot at least half an hour before you and Miss Willis and Mr. Davy came in and found him. So if Mrs. Ellison was not aware that what had wakened her was a shot, why should she have been afraid and gone on sitting on the edge of her bed for a full half hour?"

"She probably heard Mr. Peters come in," Camilla said. "If he called out, she didn't know his voice. That would have scared her, I think."

"Mr. Peters says he had been in the house only a few minutes when you returned to it."

"Well then, I don't know how to explain it," Camilla said. "But I'm sure my sister didn't shoot the man, hadn't got a gun, wouldn't have known how to use it if she'd had one, and didn't know it was a shot that woke her up."

Matthew was lighting a fresh cigarette. "Mrs. Ellison is not in a really normal state, you know, Senhor Chefe," he said. "Think of how, in her disabled condition, she depended on her husband and what his death meant to her. They were devoted to one another, besides. It was a quite unusually happy marriage. She puts on a brave enough show most of the time, but she hasn't even begun to recover. So if her behaviour isn't always that of a normal person, you shouldn't be too surprised."

"I understand that," the detective said. "It is all very sad. Now if we may return to something I asked earlier —Miss Carey, you say that in spite of your sister's condition, you intend to return to England soon? I ask just to be certain I have understood you correctly . . ."

He then went on to make certain that he had understood correctly the answer to every question that he had already asked.

Now and then he threw in a few extra ones. He repeated a number of them more than once after that. When Camilla finally left the room she felt as if she had been wrung dry of all thought and feeling. She was near to not caring what she said. It would have been a very dangerous state of mind to be in if she had had anything serious to hide from Senhor Raposo.

After her, Joanne was called in, and last Alec Davy. It was past eleven o'clock when the police finally left the house.

Before leaving, they insisted on searching it. Roberta was furious, demanding a search warrant, threatening to complain to some unknown higher authority, forgetting that she was not in her own country. Matthew calmed her down by telling her that a search was to her own advantage, for even if it was conceivable that she had possessed a gun, she could not by herself have got rid of the weapon, since she could not have left the house to dispose of it. So if it was not there, she could not be under suspicion. She saw his point and stopped her protests.

No gun was found.

By the time that the police left Roberta was so tired that Camilla tried to persuade her to go straight to bed. But Roberta's exhaustion was of the kind that made her restless. She needed a sedative, but fractiously refused to take one. She would sit down for a minute or two, saying that she was going to bed immediately, then get up, sit down in another chair, get up and limp about again. And all the time she kept talking in a high protesting voice about how horrible everyone had become recently, how they had all changed simply because she no longer had a husband to look after her.

All of a sudden Joanne, who had sensibly made some sandwiches and coffee for them all, retorted in a clear, cutting voice, "If you mean me, Mrs. Ellison, I did *not* take those ear-rings."

Roberta clapped her hands over her ears. "Oh God, oh God, have we got to start talking about *that* now?"

"Well, it's quite important to me, if not to anybody else," Joanne said. "For one thing, if you think I'm a thief, you might mention it to the police. Or you may have done that already, for all I know. Have you? I'd like to know where I stand."

"I haven't told the police anything about the ear-rings," Roberta said, "and I don't intend to, unless I must. All the same, they're gone."

"What's this about ear-rings?" Matthew asked. "No one's told me anything about them."

"It's just that they're missing," said Roberta. "My turquoise and diamond pair."

"And Mrs. Ellison thinks I took them," Joanne said. She was puzzling Camilla. Her hair was tumbled about her face, her colour was high and there was still an air of excitement, almost of exultation about her. "All the same, where are they now? The police have just searched the house."

"But not for ear-rings," Alec Davy pointed out. "It was a gun they wanted."

"This time," Joanne said. "But it wasn't much of a search, was it? Let me tell you, if they don't find the gun that man was killed with, they're going to be back, and they'll take this house apart, brick by brick."

Matthew observed her thoughtfully. "You sound experienced," he said. "Surprisingly experienced."

"It's just common sense," she answered. "Don't you think yourself they'll be back?"

"Quite likely," he agreed.

"And this time," she said with explosive anger, "they'll find those ear-rings, and they'll be in my room!"

"Joanne . . ." Christopher muttered, it might have been

94

in protest or a warning. "We're all worn out. We'd be sensible to stop discussing all these things, don't you think?"

"But I think Miss Willis is quite right," Matthew said, "the police will almost certainly be back for a much more thorough search for the weapon. That's to say, if they don't find the murderer immediately, which they may well do. An island isn't the best possible place for committing a murder. Assuming, however, that they'll be back, I think, in fairness to Miss Willis, we might try to clear up this matter of the missing ear-rings before they come. Roberta, are you sure they're missing?"

"Of course I'm sure," she said. "I hunted and hunted. I hunted for them yesterday and I hunted to-day."

"Mrs. Ellison," Alec Davy said diffidently, "I don't want to interfere, but isn't it possible you've developed a sort of blind-spot about them? It's an easy thing to do. I do it all the time. I mislay precious papers, which perhaps bore me, but which represent years of hard labour to some other poor chap, and I go through hell thinking I've lost them, and there they are on my desk, right under my nose, all the time. Don't you think something like that might have happened? I mean, you've been worried and upset. Perhaps the ear-rings are really in some quite obvious place and you've looked at them but just can't see them."

It was the perfect way out that he was offering Roberta, if she wanted to take it. The ear-rings could turn up now in any likely or unlikely place and she could greet their discovery with an embarrassed little laugh and say, "Oh dear, what a fool I've been!" Everyone would sympathise with her and forgive her.

But she seemed to have no use for a way out. With her face grey-white with fatigue, she leant towards him and hissed, "Mr. Davy, I am not a lunatic. I may be a cripple, I may have lost my husband, I may not be at my best, but I am not yet out of my mind. If someone will fetch my jewel-box for me—Camilla, perhaps you'd do it—you can see for yourself if I've got a blind spot. If the ear-rings are there, you may do what you like with them. You may keep them. You may take them to that sister of yours. If they are not there, you may search my room. You may search anywhere in the house. *You'll find that they are missing!*"

Joanne gave a short laugh of derision. "Just search my room, Mr. Davy. That's all. Search my room."

"Camilla, please," said Roberta.

Camilla went to Roberta's bedroom and fetched the papiermâché box inlaid with mother-of-pearl in which Roberta kept her jewellery, and put it down on the table in front of her. Roberta put out a hand to it, then drew it sharply back, as if God knew what terrors might be released in the world if she were to open it.

"No, I won't touch it!" she exclaimed. "If I do someone will say I took the ear-rings out here, right in front of you all, just to prove my point. Camilla, you open it."

"All right." Camilla lifted the lid.

Roberta kept her ear-rings on the middle tray in the box. She had always liked ear-rings and had a good many pairs, one of garnets, one of opals and emeralds, one of Mexican silver. There were others. And among them were the turquoise and diamond pair, which she had said were missing.

She saw them at once, went rigid as she stared, then threw back her head and began to scream with laughter.

"For God's sake, Roberta!" Matthew said.

"I'd get her to bed," said Christopher.

Joanne began to laugh too, not hysterically, but with mocking satisfaction, which gave the two women the air of sharing some tremendous secret joke together. But both went quiet again almost immediately. Too quiet. Camilla got Roberta to bed. Lying there, she clutched Camilla's hand.

"Believe me," she said in a low, hoarse voice, "I told you the truth about them. They vanished."

"Let's talk about it to-morrow," Camilla replied. "It isn't very important, anyway."

"But it is. I've got to make you believe me. She took them, don't you see, then got frightened to-night with the police everywhere, and slipped them back into the box."

"She? Joanne?" Camilla sat down on the chair by the bed.

"Of course."

"When did she put them back?"

"Any time the room was empty. It would have been easy. Listen, I'll tell you what I think happened." Roberta was speaking rapidly, with her strong fingers still gripping Camilla's hand. "That girl's a thief, I know it. I think she was in trouble at home and your friend Christopher obligingly tried to help her out of it by dumping her on me. But her own accomplices knew where she'd run off to. That man who was killed here—I think he was after her, and she shot him."

"I suppose that's as likely an explanation as any," Camilla said dubiously.

"If it's wrong, then your Christopher shot him," said Roberta. "He could be more involved with her than you've realised. Have you noticed how she's turned into a quite different person since he got here? She's suddenly become extraordinarily attractive."

"Let's talk about it to-morrow," Camilla repeated. "You're worn out and so am I."

"Stay with me a little longer," Roberta begged.

"Oh, I'll stay, but don't let's go on talking. I think I could believe almost anything about anyone to-night."

They were silent for a moment, but then Roberta went on compulsively, "I shan't trust anyone now! First Julie, now Joanne. What *am* I to do?"

"Don't worry," said Camilla. "I'll stay on here as long as you need me."

Roberta at once let go of her hand, giving it a gentle pat as it lay on the light blanket.

"No, you can't do that," she said. "You must go home. Look what's happened through my trying to keep you.

It's strange, but I always seem to bring harm to people, I don't know why. I don't mean to, but it seems to happen. Look at what happened to Justin."

"Justin?" said Camilla, puzzled.

"Yes, I really believe in my heart I killed him."

"You know that's nonsense."

"No, it's not nonsense at all. He was a dedicated surgeon. He ought never to have given it up. I oughtn't to have let him. It broke his heart, doing nothing. I saw it. I watched it. People do die of broken hearts, you know. In the same way I sometimes wonder if Moira didn't drive over that precipice on purpose because she saw what she'd done to Matthew. He's so nice, so good, but so futile. If you stayed on, the same would happen to you. I do understand that I'd slowly kill you. No, you mustn't stay. But what I told you about the ear-rings was true. They did vanish."

Camilla was almost beginning to believe her. But she had developed a splitting headache and did not know which she wanted more desperately, to go to bed and to sleep or to have half an hour alone with Christopher.

The sisters were both silent again for a few minutes, then Roberta said, "All right, I'm feeling better. Go now. Thanks for staying."

"I'll stay till you go to sleep," Camilla said.

"No, it's all right, I shan't sleep, anyway. Go and talk to him." Roberta smiled briefly. "I only wish I liked him better, Camilla. He's so smooth. Far too smooth for you. That gangly creature with the big ears would be far better for you, or Matthew, who's infatuated with you. But I suppose you think he's too old. And d'you know something else I wish? I wish I weren't such a bitch. I don't expect you believe me, but I often wish that. It would be so nice to have a nice nature. But I don't suppose I'll ever change. All in all, you put up with me pretty well. Good night, my dear."

"Good night." Camilla bent and kissed her, a thing she seldom did, and went out quietly.

The gangly creature with the big ears had already left. Joanne had gone to her room. Matthew and Christopher were still sitting over the remains of the coffee and sandwiches. They seemed to have been sitting there in silence. There was that feeling in the room. They looked like strangers in the waiting-room of a railway station, waiting for different trains, paying no attention to one another. Camilla started to pour out a cup of coffee for herself, but the pot was cold.

Matthew took it from her. "I'll make some more," he said.

As he went to the kitchen, Christopher remarked rather sourly, "He seems to know his way around the house pretty well."

"He and his wife were old friends of Justin's and Roberta's." Camilla sat down on a chair, facing him across the table. He did look smooth, she thought, and strong and resilient, like a polished, flexible rod of steel. Which might not be the most comforting thing possible to have about the place, but had its own perfection and at times would have its uses.

"I didn't realise he'd got a wife," he said.

"He hasn't. She was killed in an accident. It brought him closer to Justin and Roberta, I suppose. He's always helped Roberta a great deal."

Christopher reached out suddenly across the table and clasped both her hands in his. "When am I going to see you alone? Could you drive me down to Reid's?" he asked.

"I think I ought not to leave Roberta alone with Joanne," she answered.

"She'd be all right."

"No. She's been through too much to-day."

"But if we asked Frensham to stay here . . ."

"To-morrow," she said. "I'll come down to see you in the morning."

"No, now," he said. "You needn't be gone long. Just ask Frensham to stay while you drive me down to Reid's. We've got to talk."

She bent her aching head and rested it on his hands.

"Oh Christopher, everyone wants to talk except me," she said, "and I just want to sink down into a deep, dark silence."

He slid one of his hands out from under her head and smoothed her hair with it. "All right, we won't talk, but come," he said.

"I told you, I don't think I should."

"Ten minutes."

"Well then, ten minutes, if Matthew stays."

He did stay, and Camilla did not even have to ask it of him. When he came back with the coffee, he suggested that if she felt inclined to give Mr. Peters a lift back to his hotel, he would wait in the house till she returned. As he spoke he was watching them both with his familiar, neutral gaze, and Camilla recognised uneasily that it was the policeman in him speaking. He was simply making a little exploration into the relationship between her and Christopher. But Christopher thanked him and thanked Camilla for offering the lift, and she said that it was no trouble, and the two of them set out into the darkness.

As soon as they were in the car Christopher reached for her and held her tightly. He was going to kiss her, but before she even knew that she was going to do it, she evaded the kiss and pressed her face against his shoulder. He let her stay like that for a moment, then put a hand under her chin, and gently forced her face up till they were looking at one another.

"Wrong time," he remarked. "I'm sorry."

"*I'm* sorry," she said.

"And I've promised not to talk."

"Oh, talk if you want to." She started the car.

"It's about five minutes to Reid's, isn't it? There isn't much one can say in five minutes."

"I'll come and see you in the morning."

"As you said before. You always get your way in the end."

"I don't, I don't!" she cried. "I've been quite hopelessly

not getting my own way most of my life. I don't know what to do. If only you'd help me——"

"Instead of wanting to kiss you and remind you I'm in love with you."

"Are you? Are you? Have you ever been? Won't it happen again just as it did before? Won't you simply vanish again one day?"

"I'm here, you know," he said. "I said I'd come for you and I have."

"So it's out in the open at last."

"Well . . ." He paused, shifting slightly in his seat.

She did not mean her voice to sharpen, but she heard it happen. "Isn't it out in the open? Doesn't Helen know where you are?"

"She knows where, but I'm afraid not why. Not yet."

"I wonder if I do."

"And I wonder what that means," he said. "If it means anything. If it doesn't, just say so. I'll understand that quite well. We're neither of us exactly ourselves to-night. You were probably right, it would have been far better not to start talking at all."

The worst of it was that she did not know what she had meant. She was feeling like two people. One of them wanted to stop the car where they were, cling to Christopher, feel his mouth and his body against hers and draw love and strength and hope from them. The other person in her was thinking more or less coolly, though with a little flame of anger flickering through the coolness, that his coming here to-day was the last straw. For he knew Joanne. He had sent her to them. And it was Joanne, it had to be, who had somehow brought to Roberta's house the stranger who had got himself murdered there.

Camilla was not saying yet that Joanne had murdered him. She was not saying that Christopher had. But Christopher and this man had arrived in Funchal on the same day and she had found Christopher right beside the man's dead body. So how could it be possible that he had no connection of any kind with what had happened?

101

Weren't the coincidences piling up a little too thickly, too fast?

This second, wary person in Camilla had also another unpleasant thought at the back of her mind. She could not quite bring herself to believe that Christopher Peters would come all the way out to Madeira simply on her account. In the past few months, she had allowed herself to believe that kind of thing a few times too often and had received some good hearty kicks in the teeth. The man Christopher had become during the lost seven years of her life usually had to have three or four good reasons for taking any important step. Yielding to impulses was a luxury that he steadfastly denied himself.

"I'll come down in the morning as early as I can," she said as she turned the car in at the gateway of Reid's Hotel and drove down the short, curving drive. "If I can't, for some reason—if the police come back, or anything like that—I'll telephone."

He paused a moment before getting out of the car. "You're telling me not to come up to the house."

"Well, Roberta doesn't approve of you, and she's very near breaking-point. I think perhaps we ought to wait and see how things go."

"I see. Yes, I see." One of the hotel porters had opened the door of the car. "All right, I'll expect you in the morning. But, Cam——"

"Yes."

He hesitated. Behind him she had a glimpse through the lighted entrance of the quiet Edwardian splendours of Reid's, the deep carpets, the dignified, white-jacketed night-porter, the huge and magnificent bowl of ginger lilies in a niche facing the door.

"Just come," he said. "Don't let anything stop you, even the police. God, Cam, don't you want to?"

The two people in her wanted to give wildly different answers. She was shaken herself at how different they were and at the force with which the one wanted to answer,

"No, no, no, I dread it! It's all finished. We've only been deceiving ourselves these last few months. Whatever we once had, it's been dead and gone for years." So the whole self to which these two added up only gave a dim and tired smile and said, "Of course I do. Well, good night."

He did not answer, watching in silence from the lighted doorway as she drove off.

When she got back to the house, she found Matthew waiting in the sitting-room, reading. He had put the room to rights while she was gone, straightening furniture that had been moved by the police, erasing the remains of the chalk marks on the floor. It was characteristic of him that he should have done so, and characteristic too that he should then have sat down comfortably to read in the room where the murder had taken place.

Camilla knew that she was not going to be able to adjust herself to the situation so rapidly. For her the room would remain a place of horror for a long time to come.

He told her that while she had been gone Ione had telephoned. Somehow she had heard of the murder in the town and had declared that nothing, but nothing, would make her return to a house where everyone's life was in danger. Matthew said that he had not tried to persuade her to come.

"I thought you'd probably sooner get to bed than stay up to cope with a dose of hysteria in Portuguese," he said. "I hope I was right."

"Quite, quite right!" Camilla dropped into a chair.

"Now are you going to feel all right here if I go home, or shall I stick around?" he asked.

"We'll be all right—but thank you."

"Anything I can do, you'll let me know?"

"We always do, don't we?"

"I hope so." He smiled. "About those ear-rings of Roberta's, Camilla . . ." But something in her face checked him. "No, all right, it can wait till the morning."

"What were you going to say?"

"I was only going to ask whether or not you believed Roberta about them."

"You mean that someone stole them, then put them back?"

"I've just been wondering. But we can talk about it in the morning. Good night."

He stooped over her, gave her a quick kiss on the cheek, a good night kiss, merely to comfort and reassure, and went out. Camilla, thinking that the number of things that were to be talked about in the morning were piling up, got up, made sure that the doors and windows were locked, turned out the lights and went to bed.

However, when the morning came, as glitteringly bright as usual, there was no chance to talk of anything. By the time that Camilla had got the breakfast, taken Roberta's to her in bed, knocked on Joanne's door and told her that the coffee was ready, taken her own out on to the terrace, drunk two cups and eaten half a buttered roll, the police were back.

The Chefe had two uniformed men with him to-day, whom he left to stroll about in the road in the mounting heat of the sun while he came in, accepted a cup of coffee and talked to Camilla. As they began Joanne emerged from her room in her peach-coloured dressing-gown, leant against the door-frame and listened.

"You will be interested to hear, Miss Carey," the Chefe said, "that we have already identified the dead man. He is a Mr. Louis Pope." He spelled it for her. "And he arrived in Funchal the night before last on the cruise-ship that docked here then. The ship left Tilbury fourteen days ago, has been to Tangier, Casablanca, and the Canaries, and from here will return to Tilbury, calling only at Lisbon. His passport states that he is forty-seven, is a business executive, and people on the ship who have so far been questioned say he was a quite unremarkable man, friendly, glad to talk to people and to take part in the social activities on board. Yet he appears not to have talked much about himself, for it is surprising how little information about him his fellow-passengers have been able to give me. No one has been able to tell us what company he worked for, or even whether or not his wife was alive or dead, a question that might easily have arisen, since he was travelling without her, and unaccompanied ladies on cruise-ships are not incurious. He appears to have been sympathetic to these unaccompanied ladies, but not more than that. He was popular with them, however, even if some of them thought him reserved. His passport is a new one, so we do not know if he was in the habit of travelling, in cruise-ships or otherwise. He booked, the ship's records show, two weeks before sailing. No one remembers him saying anything of having friends here or of intending to pay any visits in Funchal. He was seen to leave the ship early in the morning . . ."

"Please, just a minute," Camilla said, as this flood of information, which seemed to tell her nothing, looked likely to flow on and on. "You said just now that no one on the ship knew if his wife was alive or dead. But how do you know that he was married at all? His passport wouldn't have shown it. It would have if he'd been a woman, because she'd have been called Miss or Mrs., but a man's simply Mr., which doesn't tell you if he's married."

"Quite correct, Miss Carey," said the Chefe. "But he had a son travelling with him, a young man of about twenty-five years of age, so it is natural to presume marriage at some stage of Mr. Pope's life. The son, unfortunately, is not to be found. He left the ship yesterday morning with his father, was seen with him at Blandy's, tasting Madeira, and in some souvenir shops, where they chose some basket work and embroideries together, no doubt as gifts to take home. They had lunch at Reid's, and then they both disappeared. We know where the father reappeared, even if so far we have discovered nothing of how or why he came here. But the son has vanished. He did not return to the ship last night and we have found no trace of him in the town this morning."

He paused to drink some coffee. As he did so Camilla became aware that the pink, lounging figure of Joanne had gone from the doorway.

The Chefe appeared not to have noticed it. He went on, "We shall soon find him, of course. A man must eat, so in spite of our mountains and our forests it is not easy to stay concealed for long on an island the area of which is less than a thousand square kilometres. And he cannot leave it, so we shall find him. Unless, of course, he has gone over the cliffs into the sea of his own free will, or assisted by a murderer. That is the one sure way of disappearing for ever from such an island as Madeira."

CHAPTER VII

CAMILLA THOUGHT of the cliffs of Madeira. They are towering and dark. There are not many harbours on the island, not many welcoming places where the ground slopes gently down to meet the water. Everywhere the stark cliffs rise straight up from a narrow rim of tumbled rock, round which the waves lick, foaming.

She said, "Don't you believe he killed his father?"

"I believe nothing," the detective answered. "I think nothing. Not yet. To me the main question still is, why did this man, this Mr. Pope, come to this house? You still have nothing to tell me about it—now that you know his name?"

"Nothing at all."

"That name means nothing?"

"Truly, nothing."

"I wonder if it also means nothing to Mrs. Ellison and Miss Willis."

"I imagine you'll want to ask them that yourself," Camilla said, "but my sister's in bed still and Miss Willis seems just to have gone to get dressed. Shall I tell my sister you want to speak to her?"

"If you'd be so kind."

She gave him some more coffee, then went to Roberta's room and told her hurriedly what she had just been told by the Chefe.

As she had expected, Roberta looked bewildered, saying "Pope?" in a voice both puzzled and mocking, as if this quite ordinary name was a peculiarly ridiculous one, the kind at which people always laugh, and as if there were something wonderfully absurd in this detective imagining that she would know any person called by it.

Camilla realised that Roberta had woken up in one of her more awkward moods. Almost anything mentioned to her would turn out to be somehow comically beneath contempt. This was unfortunate, Camilla thought, for she doubted if the Chefe was a man to take it kindly.

"Well, the Chefe wants to see you and ask you himself if you know a man called Pope," she said. "Where's your bed-jacket? I suppose you want it."

"For a policeman? But of course. I'm sure Portuguese policemen are very puritanical. It's in the cupboard."

Camilla fetched the frilly little jacket from the cupboard and helped Roberta into it.

But when Camilla returned to the terrace she discovered that the Chefe had no intention of questioning Roberta in her room. If she was able to get out of bed at all, he said, he would prefer to speak to her out here, since he wished his men to search the house once more, and if they could enter Mrs. Ellison's room fairly soon this would be of assistance.

So Joanne had been right when she said that they would be back to search again.

"But you searched the house last night," Camilla said.

He answered, "It was dark already. Besides, we were only searching for the gun that was used to kill Mr. Pope."

"What else are you searching for now?"

"I do not know. No, I truly do not know, Miss Carey. But for something. I do not know what it is, but still for something."

107

"How can you search for a thing if you don't know what it is?"

He smiled. "It would surprise you how easy that can sometimes be. I shall search for—call it some strangeness, any strangeness, that seems to fit with the strangeness of finding that dead man in this house."

"I see. But I'm afraid you'll have to wait for quite a time if you want to see my sister out here. She can't get dressed in a hurry."

"I will wait," he replied equably. "It is very pleasant here."

However, when Camilla went back to tell Roberta what he had said he did not remain on the terrace, but strolled down to the garden and walked about in it, pausing to look at bushes and clumps of flowers, much as Christopher and Joanne had done the evening before. Also, as Camilla discovered when presently she returned to the terrace with a haughtily bad-tempered Roberta, he had called the two constables in from the road and set them to poking about in the banana plantation below the garden. It was plain that what they were doing, crawling about on the ground in the shade of the great spreading fronds of the banana plants, was looking for the gun. But when Roberta appeared the Chefe called the men into the house and set them to work again, searching it.

They began with Roberta's room, then moved on into Camilla's. Meanwhile the Chefe asked Roberta if the name Pope meant anything to her.

She answered acidly, "It does not. And I must say, it seems to me most unlikely that it's his real name. A man like that would almost certainly be travelling under an assumed one."

He looked puzzled. "A man like what? One of our problems is, we do not know what sort of man he was."

"I mean a man who gets himself murdered in the house of complete strangers who've never done him any harm," she said.

"Ah. And that's your only reason for supposing Pope is a false name?"

"Of course."

"Nevertheless, you may be right," he said as he left them to direct his men in their search.

As soon as he had gone Camilla went to the telephone and rang up Reid's Hotel.

When they had put her through to Christopher's room his voice answered her frigidly, "Cam? I thought you were coming down here early. Do you know what the time is now?"

"I couldn't come," she said. "The police are here."

"The idea was, you weren't going to let anything stop you, even the police."

"That idea was yours. But I'm sorry I didn't telephone sooner."

"What the hell's the good of the telephone?" he demanded with childish irritability. "I'll tell you something, Cam—if ever I commit a murder, it's going to be with a telephone. That's the blunt instrument I'll use. Waiting for the damned thing to ring—or on some days to stop ringing—brings out all the aggression in me."

"Oh God, you're in as bad a temper as Roberta this morning," she said. "Will you listen a minute, Christopher? They've found that that man came out from England on the cruise-ship that's in just now. His name is Louis Pope. He's a business executive, whatever that is, or so his passport says, and he had his son travelling with him. The son came ashore with him yesterday morning, but now he's disappeared. I asked Senhor Raposo if he thought the son killed the father, and he said he doesn't think anything yet."

"Sons have been known to kill fathers, probably more than we ever hear of, and I expect they feel all the better for it," Christopher said callously.

"But why choose Roberta's house to do it in?"

"Didn't I suggest yesterday that that could have been an accident?"

"Oh, I know—going to the wrong address. Somehow I don't think the Chefe thinks much of that idea."

"Well, it could be—oh, you can think of all sorts of explanations, once you start trying. It could be that the father knew the son was going to try to kill him and ran into the first refuge he could find."

"They were seen having drinks and lunch together quite peaceably at Reid's."

"Perhaps the son had spells of lunacy, then. Perhaps that's why they went on the cruise in the first place, to give him a nice rest after a mental breakdown. But yesterday something snapped inside him . . ."

"Oh, Christopher—please !"

"All right," he said with a laugh, sounding better-tempered, "it's nonsense. Your friend Raposo's probably right. The central question is, why did Pope go to your sister's house? But also why, if the son didn't kill him, has he disappeared, instead of being the person who's raising hell? Cam, are you coming down here this morning?"

She could see a constable tapping on Joanne's door.

"As soon as I can," she said.

The constable had received no reply. As Christopher gave a sceptical grunt and rang off, the man came to Camilla, making gestures to ask her to go into the room to see, she supposed, if Joanne were decent and he might go in.

Camilla went to the door and knocked. There was no sound inside. She knocked again, then opened the door. There was no one in the room.

Beckoning to the policeman to come and see this for himself, Camilla left him and went looking for Joanne, in the bathroom, the kitchen and all the other rooms, and in a minute or two had made sure that she was not in the house. Returning to the terrace, she told Roberta. "She's gone."

Frowning, Roberta asked, "Who?"

"Joanne. She isn't in the house."

"But she can't have *gone*. Packed up and left. Disappeared. Don't be ridiculous."

"I didn't say she'd packed up and disappeared," Camilla said. "She hasn't. Her things are all over the room in their usual mess, but she isn't in the house. I'd better mention it to our Chefe, hadn't I?"

"If you think so, do." Roberta refused to show any interest.

Camilla went to find him. He was just going into Joanne's room himself. She told him that Miss Willis seemed to have gone out. He thanked her for the information and said that he would look into the matter. Camilla considered asking him if he would mind if she went out too, but then decided to stay until the search was finished.

She was aware that this was mainly an excuse for delaying her talk with Christopher. She had an uneasy feeling that during that talk all kinds of things were going to come out, and not only about themselves and their feelings for one another. She had begun to see dimly a shape emerging in the events of the last week or two. Only a wavering shape, an outline that turned hazy if she concentrated on it. But it was there all the same and Christopher, knowingly or unknowingly, somehow, at some point, was a part of it.

The doorbell rang. Glad of yet another excuse for delaying going to see Christopher, Camilla went to the door. Alec Davy stood there.

He shifted from one foot to the other as he spoke.

"I'd hoped I could have a talk alone with you," he said, "but there doesn't seem much chance of it with all these policemen about."

"I'm afraid not at the moment," Camilla agreed.

With the three policemen in the little house, as well as herself, Roberta and Alec Davy, it seemed packed to bursting.

"Well, it doesn't matter," he said. "It was really just to ask you to give Mrs. Ellison a message. I wanted to ask you to tell her—well, I've thought over some of the things you said to me about her, and also about that faked reference, and I wanted to say simply that I've decided to

111

stop going after her blood. And I'll go home as soon as I can. I imagine that may not be for a few days. The police here are likely to want me to stay around for a bit. But I'd like you both to know that I shan't add to your present troubles unnecessarily."

"That's very good of you," Camilla said. "But you shall have that written apology if you want it."

He shook his head. "It wouldn't mean much. I can tell Julie what you said and she'll be quite satisfied with that. She's a nice girl really, you know. Stupid and a bit undeveloped, but still a nice girl. So if you'll just give that message to your sister for me, I'll go. I'm obviously in the way here."

"Suppose you come and give her the message yourself," Camilla said.

"Better not, I think," he answered. "It would be easier for her to hear it from you. And safer too. I've a feeling that if she found she'd won her battle too easily, she might simply throw down another glove which it would be very difficult for me not to take up. And I don't enjoy a fight, you know. I have to work myself up to it, and keep on telling myself that my cause is righteous, and that nothing is ever won by running away. . . . It's appallingly exhausting. And I should very much like to enjoy my remaining few days on Madeira."

"All right." She smiled back at him. "I'll take your message."

"I expect we'll meet again before I go."

"I hope so."

"Do *you* think I'm running away?" he asked earnestly. "Do you think I've given in too easily? You see, I find anger nothing but a dreadful responsibility, not a pleasure, open or secret."

"I believe you," she said.

"I wish we could meet sometime when we didn't have to talk about murder or any other unspeakable forms of wrongdoing. But it doesn't look as if there'll be much chance of that for the present."

112

He shifted from one foot to the other once or twice more, said good-bye abruptly and left.

Camilla went to her room to fetch her swimming things. If she was calling on someone at Reid's, she thought, she might as well take advantage of a chance to swim in their beautiful private lagoon. But emerging a few minutes later, she found her departure again delayed, this time by Matthew.

He knew of the identification of the dead man and also that Joanne was missing, for one of the policemen had been in to see him to ask if he had seen her. Matthew had also heard that further inquiries about her from Roberta's nearer neighbours had led to the discovery that one of them had seen her hurrying off down the hill towards the town. Evidently she had slipped out of the house when the two constables were crawling around in the banana plantation, looking for the gun.

But had she really gone into the town, or only as far as Reid's Hotel?

Sitting on the terrace, listening to Matthew, Camilla took off her spectacles and began aimlessly polishing them. As Matthew, Roberta and the garden faded into a haze, she seemed to see Christopher's face distinctly. She concentrated on it, trying to find in those fine-boned features that had always moved her so much, the answer to the problem of where he fitted into the pattern of the last few days, to catch another glimpse of that shape that she had seen dimly emerging. But she did not know what to look for, any more than Senhor Raposo knew what to look for in this house that he was searching.

What had the detective said that he was trying to find? A strangeness. Any strangeness that seemed to fit with the strangeness of finding a dead man here.

But there was no strangeness about Christopher's face, no change of expression, nothing that she was not used to, except that now her own concentration on it made it blur and fade, so that all of a sudden she had a frightening feeling that she might never be able to evoke it again, because the truth was that she had never actually known what those pleasant features meant. They were the letters of an alphabet that she had never been able to decipher.

Matthew was saying to Roberta, "I won't rub it in now, but I was right about that girl from the start, wasn't I? I knew there was something wrong about her. I couldn't have said just why I knew it. By the pricking of my thumbs—that was all. Or perhaps I smelled her fear. It's something I'm used to noticing. She's been terrified of something, you know, ever since she got here."

"Something to do with this, perhaps," the Chefe said and advanced among them, holding the blue fibreglass suitcase with which Joanne had arrived at Funchal.

It looked, from his satisfied expression, as if he had discovered what he wanted. But when he put it down on the table and opened it, it appeared to be merely a normal suitcase, empty.

"Really! Can't you do better than that?" Roberta said contemptuously.

"We have done very well, I think," he said. "Look."

He grasped the metal rim of the suitcase and tugged at it. The rim and the whole lining of the suitcase came away from the fibreglass.

"A false bottom!" Matthew exclaimed with intense interest.

"Yes, about two inches deep."

"But nothing in it, I suppose," said Matthew.

"Nothing."

The policeman and the ex-policeman looked at one another with restrained little smiles of pleasure. The smiles were such as two doctors might have exchanged when they had successfully diagnosed one of the rarer diseases.

"Very clever of you to spot that," Matthew remarked. "Congratulations, Senhor Chefe."

"Thank you. But I should be happier still if I knew what it had contained." The Chefe fitted the lining back in place. "Money springs to mind. A good deal of money could be packed into a flat space like that."

114

"Or papers, or drugs, or jewellery."

"Certainly."

"Wouldn't money have been heavy?" Camilla asked. "I carried the suitcase at the airport and it was quite light."

"Drugs or jewellery then," said Matthew. "And she handed the stuff over to Pope, the man who arrived in Madeira on the cruise-ship—a ship that must have left England before she did—why a cumbersome arrangement like that? . . . Oh, I see. Yes, of course. The crime, the theft, must have been committed after Pope left England. He got out of the way before it just so that he couldn't be suspected of it. And that suggests that he's a man who, in the ordinary course of events, might have been suspected. A man known to have been connected in the past with crimes of this kind. A man with a record. You've been in touch with London to see if he's got a record, of course."

"Naturally," the Chefe answered. "But there has not yet been time for a reply."

"And Joanne Willis was given the job of smuggling the loot out of the country, because she hasn't got a record," Matthew was continuing with enthusiasm. Camilla had rarely seen his face so alive. "Wasn't known to have any connection with the people responsible. Had a good chance of getting as far as this without even having to open that suitcase. And she was to meet Pope here and hand the stuff over and he was going to take it on to —where does the ship call next?"

"Only at Lisbon before returning to Tilbury."

"To Lisbon then, where I suppose he had a customer waiting. But his son kills him and bolts with the booty. So all you have to do now is find him."

The Chefe shook his head slightly. "There is still a difficulty. To be precise, there are two difficulties."

"What are they?" Matthew asked.

"The first is that it seems in the highest degree unlikely that Miss Willis would have arranged to hand the stolen property, whatever its nature, over to Mr. Pope here in this house. How could she be sure she would be able to see him secretly, or else explain his arrival? A far better arrangement for them to have made would have been to meet in the town. So if you are thinking on the right lines, Mr. Frensham, something prevented that meeting, and Mr. Pope came here to find out what it was. But Miss Willis was not in the house when Mr. Pope came to it. Yesterday afternoon she went first to the swimming pool at the Tourist Club. There are witnesses to that. Then she went to visit Mr. Davy. The page-boy at the Vila Angela has confirmed that. So it looks as if she never met Mr. Pope at all, so could not have handed anything over to him, any more than murdered him. No, the person whom Mr. Pope met in this house was Mr. Peters."

"He says the man Pope was dead already when he got here," Matthew said.

"Perhaps he was, perhaps he was not," the Chefe replied calmly. "The one person who could tell us that, I believe, is Mrs. Ellison." He turned with a swift pouncing movement on Roberta. "Mrs. Ellison, I believe you know far more about this crime than you have told us. I have noticed how sounds carry in this little house. I believe you heard the shot and perhaps voices. I believe you may even know who fired the shot. If you do, let me warn you, you may be in a position of extreme danger from the murderer. So will you please tell me all that you know? Here and now. It would distress me very much to be compelled to take you down to the *Policia*."

It was a mistake to threaten Roberta. She had a great deal of natural courage, also of obstinacy, and she had been protected for so long from the unkindness of others that she did not honestly believe that she ran any risks from it. She did not believe for a moment that Senhor Raposo could possibly mean seriously to make her go to the police station.

But at least she thought it worth her while to use a little charm on him. With her eyes wide and innocently puzzled

116

and her tone plaintive, she said, "I wish I understood why you think I'm keeping anything from you. If I knew anything, *anything*, that would help clear up this horrible affair, I'd tell you at once. But what I said before is true. I was all but asleep and those fireworks were going off, getting mixed up in a sort of dream I was having, then I heard something that I thought was different——"

"The shot."

"I've told you, I don't *know*."

"But voices—you heard voices, did you not?"

"No."

"Mrs. Ellison, you say you were alone here in the house, and at least two people came to it. We know that. And one shot the other. Do you tell me this happened without any speech between them?"

"Why not?" she asked.

"It does not seem natural. And I should tell you, Mr. Pope was not shot from behind. He was facing his murderer when he was killed. So I think he would have said something first, protested, cried out."

She shook her head. "If I'd followed someone here to shoot him, I don't think I'd have given him much chance to do that. We aren't in the middle of an Elizabethan tragedy where people can't carry out their simple little murders without spouting yards of blank verse. No, I'm sorry, Senhor Chefe, but I did not hear voices. Now tell me, what was that second difficulty you mentioned?"

"Ah, that," he said. "Perhaps it is more difficult than the other. It is that Mr. Pope and his son sailed from Tilbury two weeks ago, and they booked their accommodation on the ship two weeks before that. So they had laid their plans, if Mr. Frensham's analysis of the case is correct, four weeks ago. But four weeks ago Miss Willis did not know she was coming here to you in Funchal."

"No," Roberta said. "Of course not."

"That's extraordinarily interesting," said Matthew. "Of course, they could have planned that she should come to

Funchal as an ordinary tourist, and she may merely have taken the job as it happened to crop up, just as extra cover."

"True," the Chefe said. "I must give consideration to that. And you still say, Mrs. Ellison, you heard no voices in the house yesterday afternoon—you heard no one moving about?"

"I do," Roberta said. "I heard nothing."

She stuck to that. How far the Chefe believed her was not made clear, for in the middle of it there was a distraction of some importance. Joanne and Christopher walked out together on to the terrace.

They did not look in a good mood with one another. Joanne's face was sullen, Christopher's was severe, as Camilla had seen it once or twice when he had been having words with an unsatisfactory employee. Joanne saw the suitcase on the table and stopped dead.

"So you found it," she muttered.

"Of course they found it," Christopher said impatiently. "What do you take them for?"

"But I didn't know anything about it!" she cried in a frightened voice. "Not till a few days ago when I found it open. I didn't know anything, really I didn't."

"Just a minute, please, Miss Willis," the Chefe said. "Where have you been?"

"She came to see me," Christopher answered for her. "She came to ask my advice."

"I've known him a long time," Joanne said. "He's always been good to me. When I heard you say there was a young chap on that ship called Pope—well, I needed advice, I thought. I needed someone to tell me what to do. So I went off as fast as I could to see Mr. Peters. He told me to come back here and tell you my story. He said I should have done it straight away."

"And I've come with her to make sure she does it now," Christopher said. "Go on—tell them what you told me, Joanne."

She drew a deep breath and spoke rapidly. "Look, I don't *know* anything about all this business, but I do know a Bernard Pope who's about twenty-five years old, like you said, and whose father's in business, something to do with dairy machinery, I believe, though I couldn't tell you that for sure. Bernie I've known for some time. We're friends, we sometimes go out dancing together and so on. He's a draughtsman, working for Pollard and Rumley—they're big engineering people, I expect you know them. Bernie's nice, I like him, he's got brains, but he goes with a crowd I haven't much use for. So when I went out with him it was generally just him and me, so I don't know everything about him. They were a pretty wild lot, though, some of them, that much I do know. Well . . ."

She drew another deep breath. The Chefe seemed to find it difficult to follow her swift speech and was frowning with concentration. To Camilla what Joanne said had a sound of having been rehearsed, of being reeled out now from memory, fast, in case she should forget some of it before she got to the end.

"Well," Joanne went on, "last Christmas I went to Switzerland for a week, and I said to Bernie, wasn't I lucky to be going, but wasn't it a nuisance, not having any nice luggage? I haven't travelled much, you see, not by air, and the only suitcase I had was an old one and weighed a ton. So Bernie said, 'That's all right, I'll lend you one. It's fibreglass and weighs nothing at all and I've only used it once.' So I said, 'Thanks,' and Bernie said, 'Think nothing of it,' and said he'd bring it round to me next day, which he did, and I packed my stuff into it without ever noticing there was anything queer about it, and I went, and I forgot all about giving it back to him, and he never reminded me, so I used it to come here, and that's it you've got there. Well . . ." She gave another gasp for breath.

Camilla, who was watching Christopher with deepening curiosity, thought that his unusual air of irritability covered

119

great tension, as if he were uncertain that Joanne could get through her performance without forgetting her lines.

"Well," she went on, "it was only three days ago that I spotted there was something queer about that case. I've left a few things in it, odds and ends, you know, stockings and things, and I wanted something out and I opened the case and then couldn't shut it again because that metal rim-thing seemed to have come adrift, and then when I was trying to fix it, the whole inside of the case came loose and I saw there was a sort of false bottom to it."

"I see," the Chefe said, "and was there anything in this false bottom?"

"Not a thing."

"Is that the truth?"

"Cross my heart, not a single thing," she said. "But it started me worrying. I actually felt sick with worry—d'you remember?" She turned to Roberta. "I said I wasn't feeling too good and you said it was Madeira tummy, but I knew it wasn't, it was just worry. Worrying always goes to my stomach."

The Chefe flung a sharp question at her. "Worry because there *ought* to have been something there?"

She seemed not to grasp his meaning. "Ought to have been . . . ? Oh, you mean, did I keep anything there? No, how could I, when I didn't even know it was a trick case like that? It was Bernie I started worrying about. I've always worried about him, kind of. I thought, 'What's he been getting himself into now? What's he want with a case like this? That gang he goes with, have they been smuggling, or what?' Then I thought, 'Perhaps it's something he doesn't even know about himself, or why would he lend me the case? He'd have known I could easily chance on the trick of it, just the way I did. Perhaps that lot have been making use of him,' I thought, and I worried, wondering if I ought to write to him, or what. And then—then there was the murder yesterday, and to-day you say he's here on Madeira, and I can't make any sense of that at all."

With acid in his usually agreeable voice, the Chefe said, "It is indeed puzzling."

She seemed not to notice the sarcasm. She said helplessly, "I can't understand it. It's such a funny coincidence, isn't it? I mean, I never expected him. Bernie's father coming here too . . ." Her vague and helpless look was not convincing. She was not a vague and helpless type. The Chefe made no immediate comment on her story, however. Closing the suitcase, he handed it to an *agente*, with whom he exchanged several remarks in Portuguese, then the *agente* disappeared into the house.

"Now, Miss Willis," the detective said, "I think it will be best if you come with us to the *Policia* and make a formal statement of what you have said. You may have an *Advocado*—a lawyer—if you wish one, before you say anything further. Mrs. Ellison or Mr. Frensham will be able to recommend a man in whom you can have confidence. I would advise this. My own concern at the moment is to find this Bernard Pope. Are you sure you wish to maintain your statement that you did not expect him here?"

"Of course," she said. "It's true."

"You did not come here on purpose to meet him?"

"No, how could I?"

"Then perhaps he came here on purpose to meet you."

"I don't see how he could. He must have booked already, before he ever knew I was coming."

"Then will you come with us, please?"

Camilla expected resistance. She did not know what form it would take, tears, pleading, argument, abuse. What she was unprepared for was Joanne's casual shrug of acceptance. As at other times, she appeared to be taking life as it came.

As she and the police departed together, taking the suitcase with them, Camilla thought over Joanne's story. It was not a very probable one, but if she stuck to it, it might be hard to disprove. And if she had made up her mind to it, she would stick to it. She would not be easy to break down.

"Cam," said Christopher, coming close to her, "what about a bathe now, and lunch, and the talk we were going to have this morning? Or can you leave Roberta here alone?"

"I'll see if Matthew can stay with her and get her lunch," she answered.

She spoke to Matthew, and he agreed to stay with Roberta. Camilla picked up the swimming things that she had put down earlier and she and Christopher drove off together down the hill to Reid's.

Christopher's room was on the ground floor of the hotel. He went in to change there while Camilla waited in the fabulous garden, in the shade of the tall palms. The hotel was on a promontory. Standing with her back to the building, the sea was spread out all around her. Christopher came out of his room in a few minutes, wearing swimming-trunks, sandals and a tan shirt, hanging open. He looked lean, hard-muscled and beautifully put together. He walked lightly, neatly, almost delicately. He did not start talking yet. It was in silence, as if they were happy and at peace together, that he and Camilla walked down the winding paths, between banks of blazing flowers, to the row of cabins on a lower terrace, where Camilla changed. Then they got into the lift that took them down the cliff-face to the rocky ledges below.

The lift was worked by a brown, barefooted boy in shorts and shirt, who had a serious, handsome face, not unlike that of the Chefe. On the rocks, there were more boys, some older, some in swimming-trunks, but all with the poised, compact grace of the young of Madeira, and all with the job of looking after the comfort and safety of the mainly elderly guests. For of course to be able to afford the prices of a hotel like Reid's it was generally necessary to be fairly elderly.

It was very peaceful down on the rocks, where bodies, pink and scarlet and nut-brown, lay prone in the sun, while the Atlantic, not blue, as it looked from above, but translucent green, washed softly around them.

Christopher dived cleanly and elegantly into the sea while Camilla climbed down the steps cemented to the rocks and took off from there into the calm water. He swam much better than she did and as she was without her glasses, she soon lost sight of him. The tall cliffs were only a grey blur to her. The sunbathers on the rocks were pale streaks that might have been scrawled there in chalk. The other swimmers nearer to her were fish-like creatures, curving and swooping fantastically in the enveloping green.

All that she could see accurately were a few square feet of clear water, her own arms moving lazily in it, and her toes, when she turned on her back and brought them above the surface. There she was, a little island, all by herself, a desert island, uninhabited by a mind or feelings, as Madeira itself had once been, before it was discovered by the Portuguese, Zarco.

It had been densely covered in trees then and to clear it someone had lighted a fire. But they had not allowed for the speed with which the sub-tropical undergrowth would burgeon. No sooner had an area been cleared than it turned green again, supplying fresh fuel for the flames. They had not been able to extinguish the fire for seven years.

Seven years is a long time. There had been seven years between Christopher's dropping out of Camilla's life and his reappearance, and certainly something had smouldered on in her, but just what? Love, she had thought for a long time, and longing and desperate need. But now it was more complicated. There was the beginning of a new and very disturbing understanding. Meanwhile, this cool isolation was a wonderful feeling. She wished that it could last for ever.

It came to an end when Christopher returned, with a flailing of arms and a hiss of foam, out of the blur that was the distance, and put an arm round her and swept her towards the steps. They climbed up them and picked their way among the oiled, outstretched bodies to a quiet spot and lay down there on mattresses covered in bright cotton. For a few minutes they both lay still, then Christopher raised himself on an elbow and peered down into her face.

"For God's sake, put your glasses on," he said. "I want to know that you can see me when I talk to you."

Camilla took her glasses out of her handbag and put them on.

"I think I'm a nicer person without them," she said, regretting the way that the world around her, and Christopher, came into focus. "I take more on trust."

"Not me, you don't," he said. "You've never trusted me. Not even in the old days. Why, Cam?"

"Well, I'll tell you, if you're sure you want me to."

"Go on, I do."

She still felt mindless and relaxed and glowing from her swim into solitude, and this rather oddly gave her an illusion of extreme clearheadedness.

"Well, I think I've always known you were a crook," she said. "You are, aren't you? You're deep in this thing with Joanne and the Popes."

He blinked rapidly twice, then sat up abruptly and stared out to sea.

"God Almighty," he muttered. "I thought we were going to talk about us, Cam. You and me. Our future."

"Well—isn't that a rather important part of it?"

He looked at her curiously. "Where did you get this peculiar idea?"

"You aren't denying it."

"And I'm not going to till I know where you picked it up."

"It was lying around for anyone to pick up once they started thinking about it."

"Oh, it was, was it?" He tried to make a joke of it, but his throat seemed to have gone dry. "Is that all you mean to tell me? That I'm a crook and it's obvious to all and sundry."

"Suppose you tell me one or two things first," she suggested.

124

"I'm not sure I mean to tell you anything at all."

"Well, tell me, wasn't it really because of Joanne you came out here, and not at all because of me?"

"*Joanne*?" It was as if he had never heard the name before. Then illumination seemed to come to him. "Joanne —you want me to believe you're jealous of Joanne? Cam, I've always known you've a faintly warped mind, but do you think this is quite the time for indulging fantasies? When you get at me about Helen I understand it, but *that* girl . . ."

"That girl," she said, "is attractive enough when she feels like letting anyone see it, and there's plenty of sex to her, and the way she's been playing that down is one of the interesting things about her. Matthew spotted it as soon as she got here. He said straight away that she wasn't what she seemed."

"Matthew—that's the ex-cop, isn't it, the one who watches you all the time? Have you noticed it? Either he's in love with you, or he thinks you did this crazy murder we've got on our hands. Which is it, do you think? You know him better than I do."

"We were talking about Joanne," Camilla said. "And I'm not jealous of her."

"I thought you were just explaining why it wasn't absurd that you should be."

"That was just in passing. Now listen for a minute. Joanne's in serious trouble——"

"Not so very serious," he said. "The police may hold her for a little while, it may be uncomfortable, but they've really got nothing against her."

"And that's why you made her go to them?"

"Well, I was just trying to help her. I pointed out that it isn't illegal to have a suitcase with a false bottom. And she's got an alibi for the time of the murder. She was at the Vila Angela in Davy's room."

"Oh, Christopher, listen," Camilla said. "The false bottom of that case wasn't empty when Joanne came here, and she knew it wasn't. She knew what was inside

—something that she was supposed to hand on to those two men when they got here. But somehow the thing went missing, and she found that out a day or two ago when she says she found out about the false bottom of the suitcase and got ill with worry. She really did get ill. That much is true. I realise now she was in a state of sick fear. She stayed in her room all next day, except when she went out for a short walk. Then yesterday she overheard Roberta telling me about her ear-rings having vanished and saying that she was going to call in the police and that was the last straw. Joanne felt she'd got to do something about trying to find this thing she'd lost before they started making inquiries about her and perhaps interfering with her freedom of action. And all she could think of was to search Alec Davy's room."

"Davy's—what made her think of Davy?"

"Well, he was one of the people who'd been to the house."

"So had Frensham, hadn't he? And you and your sister and that Portuguese maid of hers. You were there all the time. Why should she have picked on Davy?"

"For all I know, she'd searched through the house already without any of us noticing it. And Matthew's turn may have been next."

Christopher shook his head. "I think she probably went to see Davy for the very reason that she said she did. She told me all about it, you know. She said she felt sure that she was going to be accused of having stolen your sister's ear-rings, that Davy had warned her something like that might happen, and to go to him if she wanted help."

"But why search his room?"

"You've only his word for it that she did, haven't you?"

"I suppose so. Yes."

"And where do I come into all this?"

Camilla rolled over on the mattress. The sun on her back felt like a warm hand caressing her between the shoulder-blades. "I think that when Joanne went out for her short walk the day before yesterday, it was to send off a cable to you to tell you that the thing that had been in the suitcase was gone, so she couldn't give it to the Popes, and you thought that was so serious that you came out at once. It wasn't to fetch me home, or even to see me. It was to help Joanne search for the thing that's been lost."

Christopher said nothing for a moment, then muttered, "Of all the nonsense . . ."

"But it has to be like that," Camilla said. "There are too many coincidences otherwise. It was you who sent Joanne here. You might have sent anybody, but it happens to have been Joanne. And it wasn't by chance that those two men came here to meet her. It must have been planned weeks ago."

"How could it have been? How could I know you were going to ask me to find someone for you? The truth is, Cam, my love, I sent the very first person I could find, and I did that because I wanted you back. I'll admit I made a mistake—I should have seen Joanne would never do. But that's all I'll admit."

"All the same, if I'm right and Joanne did send that cable to you the day before yesterday," Camilla said, "the police probably know it by now."

He gave a sharp, angry sigh.

"And for this I've risked blowing everything into the open with Helen, wrecking the remains of my marriage, giving up any chance of keeping my children . . ."

He lay back on his mattress, and stretched an arm across Camilla's back and deliberately drove his nails into the flesh of her upper arm.

If they had not been in such a public place, Camilla thought, as she almost cried out at the pain, he would have done something far more violent. For a moment she had a sense of something intensely dangerous there close at her side. Then he let go of her and folded his hands under his head.

"The truth is, you've never forgiven me for what happened all those years ago," he said. "I ought to have known you couldn't. You've simply been waiting these last few months for a time when you could get back at me."

"That isn't true," Camilla said. "And I don't think it's true either that you've wrecked your marriage. I believe Helen's known about us from the first, and doesn't much care. And she knows the real reason why you came here. You've always been good partners in business."

In the silence that followed, a young girl, wet from swimming, with her long, dripping hair hanging down her back, walked past, close to them, to rejoin her family party. It was a French family. There was a mother, mostly covered up in a towelling wrap of flaming pinks and orange, with an emerald green hat on her head. The father was short, stout, very hairy and apparently asleep. A son, an elegant-looking boy of about nineteen, was reading a French translation of a James Bond novel while he massaged oil into his glistening, slim, brown limbs. The girl was about sixteen and wearing the tiniest of white bikinis. Her wet footmarks on the hot rock, as she went past Camilla and Christopher to throw herself down on one of the brightly coloured mattresses, dried almost as soon as she had made them. There was hardly a trace of them left by the time that Christopher spoke.

"There's only one thing you haven't said about me yet," he said. "Am I a murderer?"

CHAPTER VIII

CAMILLA DROPPED her head on to her folded arms. She was suddenly overcome by a feeling of extraordinary exhaustion. She felt as if each thing that she had said had been torn out of her by a physical effort, and as if the ability to say any more, or even think any more, had left her.

But she was aware of relief that Christopher had not

simply denied everything. It was an odd feeling. In a twisted way, it seemed to betoken that there was still a remnant of trust between them.

"Well?" he said.

"Well——" she began and stopped, incapable of going on.

"Suppose," he said, "—I'm not admitting anything, but just suppose—that there's some truth in what you've said, am I a murderer too?"

"I suppose not," she said.

"Why not?"

"I—don't know."

"Isn't it just that you couldn't face it? You can just face the rest, the thought that you've been kissed by a man and held in the arms of a man who's swindled and stolen—and loved him back and wanted him—but the thought of murder's too much. If I told you now I killed that man you'd feel you couldn't live with yourself and your memories. Good memories, some of them, aren't they, Cam?"

She spoke into her muffling arms. "Of course."

"But if I'm a murderer, what will happen to you? Will you have a black-out and forget it all? Forget all the past. Or perhaps forget the present, this talk, that there ever was a murder . . . You know, I'm really curious about what's going to happen to you."

Camilla was not far from a black-out of some kind just then. The little patch of the cotton mattress cover that she could see close to her eyes, within her enfolding arms, was dark and far away, as if it were the bottom of the sea at which she was gazing.

With an effort she raised her head and looked at Christopher.

"In your own way, I believe you're admitting that what I said was true."

"But the murder?" he reiterated.

"I told you, I don't know."

"So we can just forget it?"

129

"No, but——"

"But," he said, dropping his voice to a fierce whisper, "what are you going to say to other people about it, if you won't discuss it with me? And what, if you'd be so kind as to let me know, are you going to say about the rest to the police?"

"I don't know."

"Why not?"

"Because—oh, because——"

"Why don't you go straight to them and make the statement you've just made to me? Have you any doubts about it?"

"Not now," she said. "No, not now. You've practically admitted everything."

He gave a sardonic laugh. "All right. I have. You've got surprisingly near the truth. And the odd thing is, it's actually an enormous relief to talk about it. It wasn't like that at first. To begin with, when we met again, the relief was to have someone to talk to who was outside it all. It was wonderful to spend an evening with you and not plot and plan and wonder and fear."

"It seems to me we've done a good deal of plotting and planning and wondering and fearing," she said.

"But in a different way. Perhaps I have to do it. The nature of the beast. If I don't do it about one thing, I have to do it about another."

"How did it all begin?" Camilla asked uneasily. "How did you ever get into it?"

"Oh, it was years ago. It was during that time when I'd come down from Oxford—not long after I first met you—and didn't know what to do with myself. I hadn't done at all well there and that had been a great shock. I used to take for granted in those days that it was quite easy to do well at anything. I'd got through life pretty successfully so far without much effort and I was expecting a First and then a nice comfortable academic career. And I barely scraped through. So I was going to have to become a schoolmaster or some such God awful thing. So I began to have wild ideas about what I could do to avoid it. Then I met Pope."

"Is that his real name?"

"So far as I know. It's the one I always knew him by, though I don't doubt he had others to use when it was more convenient. But the whole point of this present scheme was, you see, that he, Louis Pope, well known to the police and on whom they look with something less than approval, should be on the high seas with his son Bernie, when the Countess of Engleton lost her seventy-five thousand pounds' worth of diamonds. So naturally they used their real names."

"Yes, I see. But how did you meet him? Why did you get involved with him simply because you hadn't done very well at Oxford?"

"I've told you that, haven't I? I told you, I *expected* to do well. I took it as my right. And when it didn't happen, I thought life owed me a chance to redress the balance. And Louis was the chance. I met him in a pub in Islington, a very quiet, respectable spot, just as he was himself, and we got talking. He was good at talking to strangers with a cheerful, casual, half-impertinent interest in you. You tended to take him as a joke and to tell him far more about yourself than you intended, just to keep him going, talking about himself. Of course, what he said about himself varied from person to person and pub to pub. And in a little while he knew just what sort of person you were and whether or not you were going to be any use to him. He had me spotted from the start."

"As his own sort?"

"You can put it like that. Anyway, out of a job, out of sorts and wanting money quick."

"And ready to go on with what he wanted from you even after you started to have money. That five thousand that Helen's mother left her . . . ?"

"There was no five thousand pounds. If there had been, perhaps there'd have been no more Louis in our lives. But I'm not sure. I think perhaps there's a real streak of delinquency in me—or what you could still just call delinquency then. By now it's plain criminality, that's all there is to it. No, those five thousand pounds came from jobs I'd done for Louis."

"You mean you've enjoyed working with him?"

He smiled. They had dropped into an oddly friendly, intimate way of talking, more like the way in which they had been able to talk to one another seven years ago than ever in their recent meetings.

"It's had its moments," he said.

"But what did you actually do?"

He drew a fingernail delicately down her spine. He was gentle this time.

"You're rather enjoying this, aren't you, Cam? It's quite a thrill for you."

"Well, I suppose I'm rather horridly interested."

"Take care, that's how it began for me—I was horridly interested. It's a good phrase. He talked more and more and I was fascinated and he drew me into his circle, and he knew I wouldn't give him away, because of that fascination—as you won't give me away, you see. I know that now. I oughtn't to have asked you what you were going to do. I ought to have recognised the symptoms of that horrid interest."

She twisted round on her mattress, sitting up abruptly.

"I've told you, I don't know what I'm going to do."

"But I think I do. Now where was I? Oh yes, what did I actually do for Louis? Well, I drove the get-away car a few times. I'm a very good driver, you know, and a good mechanic. I was useful in an all round way. I remember I provided alibis once or twice. I was never in on any of the burglaries. He didn't think I'd be up to it. I hadn't the background. But I made quite a bit of money, and the time came when Helen and I thought we'd pull out. And that's where we found we'd made our big mistake, of course, because you can't ever quite pull out from people like Louis."

"Blackmail?" she asked.

"Not quite as crude as that. More a little help expected of

us now and then for old times' sake. Not with money, usually. Louis and his friends had a good deal more than I had. But the occasional quiet meeting in one of our upstairs rooms from time to time, and the occasional alibi. And, of course, information. By degrees, you see, through our work, Helen and I began to be the kind of people who have a great deal of information. I began to know a surprising amount about a number of pretty wealthy people. That's when Louis's early interest in me, which looked almost like charity at the time, began to pay off for him. He was a shrewd old coot, Louis was. He knew more about me, as they say, than I did myself. He'd always known it would pay off sooner or later."

"So after all," Camilla said thoughtfully, "you'd a very strong motive for following him here and murdering him."

"I thought we'd agreed I didn't murder him."

"But you *had* a motive."

"All right, I had."

"And you sent Joanne to us, with all that jewellery in her suitcase, to hand over to him when he landed here."

"The diamonds—just the diamonds. They were taken out of their settings straight away and made up into a few convenient little parcels for her. Then he was going to take them on to a customer in Lisbon."

"But you sent her here to us, knowing just what she was."

"Yes, and Julie."

"*Julie*——?" For the first time since they had started talking, he had completely startled her. All that he had told her about himself so far had in some obscure way fitted together, like the pieces of a difficult jig-saw, to make a pattern which she recognised as one that she had known for a long time.

He gave his quiet, pleasant laugh. "Of course."

"But—no, that doesn't make sense, Christopher. Louis and Bernie weren't on the high seas when Julie came to us. She came weeks ago. They were still in England. The burglary hadn't even happened. No, I don't believe you, Christopher. You're making it up to confuse me."

He shook his head. "Julie was in it all right. She was, so to speak, keeping the place warm for Joanne. I knew you were coming here, you see, and you'd told me you'd soon be advertising for a companion for your sister, so when the advertisement appeared, we answered it. That reference from the bishop—I wrote it myself. I was rather proud of it."

"But suppose she hadn't got the job, in spite of the reference."

"Then we could have dropped the whole scheme. It was only after Julie'd got the job that Louis and Bernie booked on the cruise. The burglary itself, of course, was carried out later by some of Louis's boys. Then the diamonds were brought out here by Joanne, who'd done a few little messenger jobs for them already, but hadn't been suspected of it, to the best of our knowledge. Only a job like that couldn't get set up immediately. It needed preparation, though the main outline had been worked out quite a long time before. And there was the risk that your advertisement would get answered straight away by someone who was longing for a nice long stay on Madeira and we'd never get our chance of sending Joanne here after the jewellery had been stolen. She could have come as an ordinary tourist, of course, but she'd have been rather more conspicuous. Coming to a job with a respected resident of Funchal seemed a far better cover. So we sent Julie, to keep the job waiting."

"How did you get to know her?"

"Louis found her, more or less as he found me. She'd been sacked from a job for some minor dishonesty and was pretty bitter about everything. And this was a nice easy little job to try her out on. All she had to do was behave perfectly until she got a telegram from home, telling her to return at once, in time for you to do what we thought you'd do—ask me to find someone for you. If you hadn't done that, of course, I'd have rung you up and put the idea into your head. I was just getting ready to do it when you rang me. That's why I sounded so astonished. Things were working out almost too well. We didn't have to send a telegram to Julie. Your sister wanted to get rid of her anyhow, to keep you here. But haven't you ever wondered why Julie went so quietly, without trying to justify herself and prove that your sister's accusations weren't true?"

Camilla sat up, drawing her knees up and resting her chin on them. She gazed out to sea.

"And Alec Davy?" she asked. "Is he in on all of this too?"

Christopher did not answer. At last she looked round at him and found him looking up at her with a smile that had both mockery and sympathy in it.

"Poor Cam," he said, "taking everyone at their face value."

"Not after to-day," she said. "Never again."

"Of course he's in on it," he said. "I'm sorry. But knight errants don't go charging about the earth any more, standing up for the honour of damsels in distress. As a matter of fact, I doubt if they ever did. I'm sure they always did it for the loot they'd pick up on the way. But Davy isn't in with us. He's in it strictly for himself. He must have got Julie to tell him the real reason why she came to Madeira, though there must have been some slip-up there, because she wasn't supposed to know any details about the burglary or the jewellery. But when he found it out, I suppose he thought there was no reason why he shouldn't come to Funchal ahead of Louis and Bernie and lighten Joanne's luggage for her. I imagine he didn't find it too difficult. Apart from picking her up on the plane from Lisbon, he'd a perfectly good excuse for calling on Roberta and getting to know the lie of the land—which room was Joanne's, when you all went out, how little you bothered to lock up, and so on."

"You're only guessing. You don't know that that's why he came."

"Well, all right, if that's how you want it."

"But when Joanne found the diamonds were gone—knowing Julie's part in the business and that he was Julie's brother—the first thing she thought of was to search his room at the Vila Angela."

"Naturally. She was terrified, of course, of having to face Louis without the diamonds. When she saw he was dead, she was enormously thankful—delighted—until she remembered she'd still got Bernie to deal with. That made her decide to take shelter with the police. But if you ask me, Davy had a better motive for murdering Louis than anyone else. He admits he saw him come off the ship. Well, he could have been watching for him, and followed him about the town until he found a good spot for doing him in, and what could be better than your sister's sitting-room?"

Camilla had turned away from Christopher again and was idly watching the swooping flight of a swallow high above the rocks on which they lay. It was an odd thing about swallows, she thought, the way that some of them spent their summers on Madeira and others went far North, at least as far as Scotland. What decided them? Were they inescapably bound to return to the place where they had been born, or had they any choice in the matter? Was your destiny fixed from birth? Christopher had said, the nature of the beast. Was that all there was to it? Had he ever had any freedom of choice in becoming what he was? Had she had any choice when she fell in love with him? And what choices, if any, were there left for either of them?

"What are you thinking about, Cam?" Christopher asked.

She took a moment to answer, "I was wondering why you've told me all this now."

He flung his arms wide on the rock. It had the look of a gesture of complete surrender. "I don't know, but I feel better at this moment than I've felt for months! You seemed to know it all, anyway."

"But suppose I go to the police."

"I don't think you will."

"I haven't promised anything."

"But you realise, of course, this conversation has never actually taken place. If you were to tell anyone about it, I should simply deny it all. That cable from Joanne —you don't think there was anything about diamonds in it, do you? We had a prearranged, innocuous message, in case anything went wrong, which meant, 'Come at once.' But that's all. No. I think I'm in the clear, unless Joanne herself talks, and I don't think she will. A stubborn girl, that—very tough. Now what about another swim?"

It seemed as good an idea as any. Camilla stood up, took off her spectacles, put them into her handbag, pulled on her bathing cap and picked her way across the rocks between the recumbent bodies of British, French, Americans and Germans to the steps leading down into the water.

As she pushed off from the steps, Christopher dived cleanly into the water from the springboard and came swimming after her with a neat, powerful flailing of arms and legs. Out of the green blur around her his face suddenly emerged, laughing, then he put both hands round her throat and pushed her down under the surface. Down and down.

It felt as if they must be going to the very bottom. She panicked crazily. She had not had time to take a deep breath before he pushed her under. The water stung in her nose and her throat. Her lungs felt like bursting. She fought with fury, but the water seemed to fight back at her. It held her in a strong, sure grasp, which made her struggling futile. At the back of her mind, behind her terror, was utter incredulity. This can't be happening, she thought with a mad sort of lucidity, not with all those handsome Portuguese lifeguards looking on, not with all the British and French and Americans and Germans happily basking in the sun. No one could try to drown you here, within easy calling distance of the shore.

Only she couldn't call.

Yet suddenly she found herself bobbing up through the water into daylight and heard Christopher laughing as he swam away from her. It had only been play. Cruel play, of course. She was still gasping and felt dizzy with the remnants of her fear. And she felt that she had been intended to recognise the cruelty, to sense the threat in it. But no one else seemed to have noticed anything amiss.

In fact, no one seemed to have noticed anything, except a small boy, swimming like a fish near her, who crowed with laughter at her ducking and tried to join in the fun by splashing her as hard as he could. She swam away from him back to the ladder and climbed up on to the rocks.

She did not wait for Christopher to return but put on her glasses, picked up her belongings and went to the lift, which took her up the cliff face, then she went to her cabin, dressed and walked up from terrace to terrace, between the banks of gorgeous flowers, to the hotel. Taking the path round it, she went to Roberta's car, got in and turned the ignition key.

It was only then that she started to shake. She began to tremble all over. It was not only the aftermath of her irrational fear hitting her, but the stress of that long, quiet talk. She sat there looking blindly ahead at the brilliant sunshine, and shivered with the chill of the cool, strong water pressing in on her. She drew several deep breaths, and still with that cold, inner trembling, started the car and drove it up the short semi-circular drive and out through the gates. She reached the bottom of the road leading up to the Ellisons' house and turned up the hill.

But as soon as she had turned the corner, she stopped the car, and sat there for a moment, thinking. Then she reversed back into the main road and drove towards the town, to the Vila Angela.

She knew that it was likely that Alec Davy might be out on one of the long walks that he enjoyed, or else already at lunch. But if she had the luck to find him and be able to talk to him at once, it might ease the tension of her nerves a little. Alternatively, of course, it might make it worse. But at least it should have the effect of dispelling some of the fog in her mind. She parked the car near the door in the high wall round the Vila Angela and went in.

She found Alec Davy in the garden. He was reading a newspaper and had a glass of beer on the broad arm of his basket chair. He did not see her till she was standing right in front of him. Then he made a startled noise and came lurching clumsily to his feet, his ears growing pink. Surely, Camilla thought, a crook, a man who would steal diamonds and do murder, couldn't afford to have ears that turned pink whenever he was taken by surprise.

She said, "Mr. Davy, have you got time now to come out for that walk round the harbour?"

"Yes—yes, of course," he said. "Yes, that's splendid." He folded the newspaper hastily into an untidy bundle and dropped it on to the chair. Then he seemed to find something disagreeable about this sight, picked up the paper again, refolded it with meticulous care and laid it down again.

"Do finish your beer," Camilla said, as he appeared to be about to start for the door in the wall, leaving his glass half full.

"Oh—oh yes—thanks." He drained the glass. "But do you really want to go wandering round the harbour? You want to talk to me, don't you? Something's happened. You look different. We could go down into the town and have lunch somewhere. Mightn't that be better?"

"It might," she said. "Yes, let's do that."

"We'll be followed, of course, but I don't suppose you mind that."

"Followed?"

"Yes, haven't you had someone trailing around behind you to-day? I have. A small, brown man in a taxi. Incidentally, have you ever seen a town with so many taxis in it as Funchal? You've only to waggle a finger without thinking and one pops out of the ground in front of you. I almost didn't notice this one that was always a little way behind me among the hundreds of others, but by degrees the man's face began to seem familiar and I got the uncomfortable feeling he was someone I ought to know and say hallo to—a colleague or a former student of mine perhaps—one's always meeting them in the most unlikely places, doing the most unlikely things, and they come in all ages and sizes and colours and nationalities, so one's never entirely safe. Well then, I realised he looked familiar only because I'd kept on seeing him all the morning. He was right behind me when I came up to see you. I almost asked him for a lift down the hill. I don't think it would have worried him if I had. He wasn't trying to be inconspicuous. . . . Look, there he is now."

They had gone out through the door in the wall and were walking towards the car. Camilla saw now what she had not noticed when she parked it, but remembered to have seen, a taxi waiting about a dozen paces from the door. There were two men in the taxi, both lounging inside it, smoking and chatting. When Camilla and Alec Davy emerged from the Vila Angela one of the men got out of the taxi in a leisurely way, got into the driver's seat and started the engine.

"I hope you don't mind," Alec Davy said in a tone of apology, as if their follower were somehow his fault. "Incidentally, while I was out this morning someone made a very neat and competent job of searching my room. It was the police this time, of course. I almost didn't notice it. When I did I began by feeling furious. I felt that sort of raging resentment one always does if a customs officer decides to make one open one's suitcases and paws through one's things. However polite the poor chap is in doing his job, one feels it's an utterly outrageous invasion of one's most private life. But then I decided to be grateful that whoever did the job had left everything so tidy, not like that awful mess I had to clear up after our friend Joanne had had her go. . . . Camilla, I'm sorry I'm talking so much." They had got into the car and Camilla had started it. "It's your face. Something's happened to you and you rather scare me. I've a way of talking too much when I'm scared."

They moved out into the traffic in the Avenida do Infante. In the driving mirror Camilla saw the taxi move out from the kerb and follow along about a dozen paces behind them.

"Where shall we go for lunch?" he asked. "I expect you can pick a place far better than I can."

"I shouldn't think so," she said. "Roberta doesn't often eat out."

"Well, there's a place I found a day or two ago. It isn't anything much, but it's quiet. I'm not sure of its name, but I think I can find it again."

He directed her, after they had passed the glittering fountain at the bottom of the avenue, on through the town, past the Botanic Garden and the statue of Zarco and the small shady square where the elderly flower-sellers sit with little round felt hats on their grey hair and short orange capes round their shoulders, as colourful themselves as the baskets of flowers before them, and finally to a small restaurant in a side-street. All the way the taxi stayed about the same distance behind them.

"I can imagine how you'd almost get to like having them there after a bit," Alec Davy said as he and Camilla got out of the car and walked towards the door of the restaurant. "You could have a sort of insulted feeling if they stopped thinking it was worth their while to tag along. Is this place all right?"

"Of course."

It was small and unpretentious, with a very scrubbed look and white curtains at the windows. They had a meal of a rather coarse kind of white fish, cooked with a sharp, lemon sauce, bread, salad and fresh figs and drank a light, rather sickly, pink wine with it.

Alec Davy ate with a good appetite, but Camilla pushed the food around on her plate and wondered what she had thought that she could say to him. His own flood of nervous talk had suddenly run out. He did not look her in the face, but when he was not looking at his plate, frowned heavily at a spot on the wall behind her.

At last she said, "It's about Julie."

"No!" he said explosively. "We've gone into that. There's nothing more to be said. I'm going to explain the situation to her when I get home and that's going to be the end of the matter."

"This is something different," Camilla said. "Something I've been told to-day. I think you ought to know about it."

He gave a worried shake of his head, as if he were trying to shake water out of his prominent ears. "Have we got to go into it, whatever it is?"

"I think you might be sorry if we didn't."

"All right, what is it?"

"I've been told that Julie knew Louis Pope."

"Pope? The man who . . . ? That man . . . ?"

"Who got murdered," said Camilla.

"Yes. No. Of course she didn't know him. How could she?"

"I think she did. And if it comes out, you're going to find you're involved too."

He rubbed one side of his jaw with his knuckles. "I suppose at a time like this almost anything may get said. Can you tell me more exactly what you've heard?"

"Well, do you know about the false bottom in Joanne's suitcase?"

"No."

She told him about it. She told him of Joanne's disappearance and reappearance presently with Christopher, how she had explained her possession of a suitcase with a false bottom and been taken away by the police to make an official statement. She went on to tell him most of what Christopher had told her that morning, though she could not bring herself to say explicitly that it was from him that she had heard it all. It came out as a story mainly of remarkable deduction and guesswork on the part of Senhor Raposo. Perhaps that was why Alec Davy seemed less impressed by it than she had expected. At the end he was smiling.

"And now I've got the swag, have I? Swag—I expect that's an archaic word, but my mind tends to run a bit behind the times. You know, I think there's a lot to be said for concentrating on what went on several thousand years ago instead of on what's going on around one now. There's something tremendously exhilarating about the detective work you can do on a few small fragments of mosaic pavement, but this kind of mosaic, these little bits and pieces of human behaviour—you can keep it. Suppose we talk about something else."

"But, Alec, this is serious. Besides, I'm not sure that I can talk about anything else. I'm not sure I can think about anything else, even if I try. I keep wondering, for one thing, what happened to those diamonds. Who did take them out of Joanne's suitcase?"

"If I didn't?"

"Yes."

"Why do you think I didn't?" he asked.

"Well . . ." She smiled. "It was you who told us that you hadn't an uncle who was a bishop. Would you have done that, would you have given your sister away like that, if you weren't honest yourself?"

"Well, it would certainly have been a fairly stupid thing to do."

"Who took the jewellery, then?"

"Perhaps Joanne herself," he said. "Otherwise, probably you, or your sister, or Frensham. I back your sister myself. She's an unscrupulous character, even if nice-natured people like us have decided we mustn't be too hard on her on that account. And she could have been rootling around in Joanne's room, looking for a good place to plant those ear-rings, so as to have a reason for getting rid of her, when she happened on the trick of that suitcase and found the diamonds." He paused and nodded appreciatively at his own idea. "That's neat, you know—that's an excellent explanation—that it was when she was looking for a good place to hide the ear-rings that she looked inside the case and chanced on the way it worked. If it weren't for that, perhaps I'd back Frensham, but why should he think of stealing the ear-rings? That doesn't seem his style, somehow. The other stuff, yes—I can see him going off with that. The temptation could be enormous, and it's often said, isn't it, that there's a very thin dividing line between policemen and crooks? But why take a pair of your sister's ear-rings? Also, I can imagine he didn't much like Joanne, but would he be so passionately anxious to get rid of her that he'd steal the ear-rings and put them in her room? And if it wasn't like that, why should he take it into his head, out of the blue, to search her room? Because that's what someone seems to have done. Out of the blue, someone searched Joanne's room and found all those lovely diamonds. . . ." He had grown thoughtful while he was talking and as he finished his gaze was again on the spot on the wall behind Camilla.

"But don't you understand what I've been saying?" Camilla said. "If Julie knew the Popes and told you about everything, then you could have known where the diamonds were all the time and known exactly where to go and look for them? It wouldn't have been out of the blue at all."

He seemed not to hear her.

"Lovely diamonds, lovely money," he murmured. "I wonder what I'd do if I suddenly had lots and lots of lovely money. Untraceable. Untaxable. What would I do with it?"

"Hide it first," Camilla said. "And that lets Roberta out, you see. The police have searched that house twice and they haven't found any trace of diamonds or the gun. And she couldn't have gone out to hide them."

"She behaved pretty oddly, all the same, after the murder, just sitting there and waiting for something to happen. Perhaps there's some wonderfully secret hiding-place in the house that nobody's thought of yet. But really what I meant when I said what would I do if I had lots of money, was what would I spend it on? I've never gone in much for daydreams in that direction. Have you? My daydreams always have to have a touch of probability about them."

"Alec, you're awfully hard to keep to the point, aren't you?" She drank some of the chilled, pretty-looking, tasteless wine. "Don't you understand you may be going to find yourself in trouble, particularly if the police found a few of the diamonds in your room while they were making their beautiful, tidy search. Because that's what Joanne could have been doing in your room the other day, you know—not searching it, but hiding one or two diamonds there to incriminate you."

To her surprise, he burst out laughing. "How nice you are—how awfully nice. And we could go on playing this game of Hunt the Murderer for ever, couldn't we? Of finding many clues there is no end . . . But what's worrying me is that I honestly don't know what I'd do with an enormous sum of money if it suddenly got into my hands. And that's a very odd thing to discover. I wonder if my imagination is much more inhibited than most people's, or if it's true of more people than realise it. I'd like to own a yacht, I think, but nothing luxurious—a five ton sloop would do me. And I'd like a nice house, but I'd hate to have servants round me to run it, even supposing they were obtainable, so perhaps a modest flat would suit me better. And I'm not much interested in cars, or fine raiment, and I aspire to a wife, rather than to expensive mistresses. And I'd enjoy the best in food and drink and I'd be reasonably hospitable to my friends, but I wouldn't be any Timon, spending all my substance on them. And horses bore me stiff and I've never in my life won anything gambling, so that's never gained any hold on me. God, this is grim! What *would* I do with a lot of money?"

"Couldn't you finance an archaeological dig or something?" Camilla suggested.

"God forbid! Use my own money when there are Government Departments and this and that Foundation whose job it is to provide adequate grants. Oh no, I'm a product of my generation, I think someone else should generally pay for the serious things of life. But it's rather a shock to discover how little I dream about money. Because that's all I'm talking about—dreams. And in terms of dreams, it's quite important to know the answer to a lot of preposterous questions."

"What *do* you dream about?" she asked.

"Success and women. Professional success and nice, kind women. Which means, for the last day or two, quite a lot about you."

She laughed. "Well, there's the answer to your problem, because I should come terribly expensive. In *my* dreams I'm a *very* expensive woman."

He looked oddly put out. "Don't laugh at me. I know I clown, but I usually mean most of what I say."

"And I'm not very kind. Look how hard I find it to be kind to Roberta."

"And look at the trouble you've taken to come and warn me about what may be in store for me if the police found any of the diamonds in my room. But if they did, why are they letting me go around loose?"

"Your little brown man is following you, isn't he?"

"Perhaps he's waiting to see if Bernie Pope makes contact with me. Incidentally, have I managed to convince you that I wouldn't steal a lot of money because I shouldn't know what to do with it once I had it?"

"No," Camilla said.

"I was afraid I hadn't." He signalled to the waiter for the bill. "Of course I know exactly what I'd do with it. I'd fritter it away. It would go on this and that without my noticing till it was all gone and I was back where I started. But thank you for coming to warn me. It was kind and nice, whatever you think of yourself."

"I'm not sure my motive for coming was in the least kind or nice," she said. "In fact, it wasn't."

Mainly she had come to talk about the stolen diamonds

and the murder and see, in the light of Christopher's accusation, how Alec Davy reacted. And after all this talking, after the pleasant lunch together, with his constant, tricky evasion of seriousness, she felt neither more nor less faith in him than she had when she called for him at the Vila Angela.

But Christopher had seen to it that faith in another human being would have a hard time taking root in her nature. Her mind had become a weedy patch of suspicions and distrust, which sprouted at fantastic speed, died and toppled over, only to be overgrown at once by others. Perhaps it would take another seven year fire to clear the ground of them and leave it fit for cultivation.

"I wonder if Little Brown Man has managed to have any lunch," she said as she and Alec rose from the table, "or if he's had to sit out there watching this door all the time."

"There you are, worrying about him, being kind again," Alec said. "It might become a habit if you were more often in the company of other kind people. You haven't actually seen very much in the way of kindness, have you? Your friends and relations strike me as people who expect a good deal without thinking they need to give much in return. You probably think you're the same without having gone at all deeply into the question. . . . Look, there he is still."

They were standing in the doorway of the restaurant, blinking against the sudden brilliance of the sun. The taxi with the two men inside it was parked about a dozen paces behind Roberta's car. The men were smoking and playing some sort of card-game. When Camilla and Alec appeared, the small dark man collected the cards reluctantly and pocketed them, while the driver got out of the taxi and back into the driver's seat.

"Where shall I drop you?" Camilla asked as she and Alec got into the car. "Do you want to go back to the Vila Angela?"

"Yes please, if you don't mind," he said. "It'll be interesting to see, when you drop me, if Brown Man sticks with me or follows you."

"I think he belongs to you. I don't think I've had anyone following me."

They were silent after that until she put him down at the door in the wall of the Vila Angela.

She had been right that the man in the taxi had no interest in her. When she drove on again it stayed behind in a patch of shade not far from the door. She drove unusually slowly, partly because she was looking in the mirror to see if any other taxi or car were following her, and partly out of reluctance to return to the house and Roberta.

After a minute or two she came to the conclusion that she was not being followed, but the reluctance to go home remained. Roberta would probably attack her for having been gone so long, would want to know in detail what she had been doing, and would make disparaging remarks about Christopher, which would hurt now as they never had before.

Camilla took the hill slowly and when she stopped at the opening to the vine-covered arch, sat still for a moment, resting her elbows on the wheel. Pressing her fists against her temples, she wondered how long it took to fall out of love, the whole way out, and to stop feeling the bruises of the fall. A life-time?

With a sigh that turned into a yawn of nervous weariness she got out of the car and went into the house.

Again a pair of feet were the first things that she saw through the open door of the sitting-room, sprawled apart, just as they had been before. But this time they were small feet in low-heeled white shoes, familiar feet attached to a pair of pitifully wasted legs in fine nylon stockings. Roberta's feet.

She was lying in the middle of the floor, as Louis Pope had lain, her eyes staring and her face grey-yellow in death. The top of her black and white linen dress was smothered in blood. There was a sickening buzzing of flies in the air.

A cry erupted from Camilla's throat without her being aware of it, and just as had happened before, a hand was immediately clamped over her mouth. But this hand was not gentle as Christopher's had been. It pressed her head back, while another hand took hold of her from behind at the base of the neck. Unable to move her head, she rolled her eyes sideways and saw a long, bony, young face close to hers. It was framed in a shock of tumbled golden hair, and had sunken grey eyes that were full of fear and anger. Golden stubble sprouted on the long, cleft chin.

"Don't give any trouble," the young man said. "We're getting out of here right now, you and me. And if you talk sense, maybe you won't end up the way she did. Come on now, move."

CHAPTER IX

As she moved obediently, helpless in his grasp, Camilla carried with her a picture of what she had seen in her brief glimpse of Roberta, lying there in her home in a dreadful solitariness.

The picture was not only of Roberta. It was of her crutches, flung out on either side of her, out of her reach, of a small table and a vase of flowers overturned by her fall, of a rug, crumpled under her. A scene of swift and sudden violence. And something was missing.

What?

Absurd to worry about such a thing at such a time. Absurd to think anything like that could matter. Yet the puzzle of it nagged at Camilla's mind like a burning headache.

As the young man released his grip of her and instead of it pressed something small and hard into her back, told her to get into the car, got in beside her and told her to drive, she felt a complete certainty that something that she was used to and ought to have seen, even in the few moments that she had been in the house, was gone. But when she tried to fight off the fog of fear to see clearly what this thing was, nothing crystallised in her mind.

Perhaps, she thought, it was simply Roberta herself, her life, her spirit. For the thing on the floor was not Roberta. Perhaps this was how grief and shock affected you when you were frightened enough for yourself. Perhaps all that you were capable of feeling was this confused sense of loss.

"Go on, drive," the young man said.

"Where?" she asked.

"Anywhere. Up the hill. Out of the town."

"What do you want me for?"

"You've got to tell me some things."

"Why not here?"

"Because I'm getting out of here as fast as I can. Now get on, get moving! And don't try anything funny."

He was holding the gun loosely on his lap, but it was still aimed in her direction, and from what she had seen in the house Camilla understood that he would not be afraid to use it. "We want to go where we won't be interrupted."

The car was already pointed up the hill. She started it and drove straight on. Still trying to think of what had been missing from the house, as if solving this would help her to keep some hold on the normal world where things like this did not happen, she realised that of course Matthew had been missing. Was that it? It was curious, in any case, that he should not have been there. He had agreed to stay with Roberta till Camilla came home. But perhaps he had not been missing. Perhaps he happened to be merely in another room, or on the terrace, where she had not seen him, dead like Roberta.

They drove up the road that went past the British Country Club and the Football Stadium. It climbed rapidly, as all roads do on Madeira, except for those that run parallel to the sea. The surface was of the usual dark rectangular cobbles, each one slightly tilted, to provide firm footholds for those walking down the steep slopes, but for driving on a misery. Once or twice Camilla tried to speak, but the young man only said, "Quiet, I tell you! I'm thinking."

What, she wondered, was thought in the head of a young animal like this? When he used the word thinking, what did he suppose it meant?

She had had time to take in the fact that he was handsome in a way, if you did not mind the long, shaggy hair and the little rosebud mouth, which showed rather rabbity teeth when the lips parted. He was tall, wide-shouldered, narrow-hipped, with a look of springy, elastic strength about him. If the hand on the gun in his lap looked relaxed, she did not doubt that it could tighten in a flash. He wore narrow black trousers, a black and yellow checked shirt and red espadrilles. Yesterday, perhaps, they had all looked clean and smart, but to-day they looked as if he had slept in them, and he smelled rankly.

All of a sudden, without knowing that it was going to happen, Camilla found herself screaming at him, "Why did you have to kill her? Why?"

He gave a violent start, as if his thoughts had been far away.

"*Kill* her?" he said.

"She was helpless, wasn't she? She couldn't have stopped you looking for what you wanted. Why did you have to shoot her?"

"Shoot her?" he said in the same stupid way. "Look, what are you talking about? I haven't killed anybody."

"You killed my sister. You killed your father. For all I know, you killed Matthew Frensham."

"Who's he?" he asked.

"The man who was with my sister."

"There wasn't any man with your sister, if that's who she was. If she was, I'm sorry. You and me both, we've lost someone, me my old man, you your sister. Too bad. We'd better both be doing some thinking."

"You killed her," Camilla said stubbornly. "That gun you've got there is the one you did it with."

"Look, I told you, I never killed anybody," he said. "I've never held with violence, there's no percentage in it —what I believe in is using my loaf. And my old man said the same. And it's what I'd be doing now if you'd shut your mouth. How can I think when you keep on talking?"

"If you don't hold with violence, why are you carrying a gun around with you?" she asked.

"Well, wouldn't you have picked it up if you'd found yourself alone in a house with a dead woman and you heard someone coming in? Turned out it was only you, but it could have been anyone."

"Do you mean that gun was there in that room with my sister?"

"That's right. Right by her hand."

"You're telling me she committed suicide."

"That's how it looked to me."

"I don't believe it."

"That's your privilege."

"If you're telling the truth, you were a fool not to leave the gun where it was," she said.

"Think I don't know that now? Now I'm trying to think. Keep quiet."

They drove on for a while in silence.

Camilla wondered if Bernie Pope had yet noticed the car behind them. It was a white Volkswagen, which she had not noticed herself until she had been driving for some minutes. When Bernie had hustled her out of the house and made her drive away she had been in too great a state of shock to be aware of anything but that picture of what she had just seen in the sitting-room, and of the young man close to her, and the pressure of the gun-barrel against her back. Whether the Volkswagen had been there in the road near the house at the time and had started to follow immediately, or whether it had come in from some side road and was following on behind merely because it happened to be going in the same direction, was something of which she could not be sure.

She did not know either how to find out which it was. If she slowed down slightly, the Volkswagen slowed down, maintaining the same fifteen yards or so between them. But what driver wouldn't on a road like this? It was not a road on which any sane driver would try to pass another car. It was too narrow, too winding, and all the time climbed up and up, with no more side roads turning off it, now that the town had been left behind.

Presently the road entered thick pine woods. Along its edges bloomed great clumps of agapanthus and as the road climbed higher still, there were groves of hydrangeas too, pale blue and creamy white. Camilla knew it as a road of great beauty, though one that had frightened her when she was driving, even when her nerves were in a normal state, for presently it would wind along the edge of deep gorges, sheer precipices, perhaps with patches of cloud to shroud them. If Bernie Pope had given her more time to think, she might not have come this way, but have taken the gentler road eastwards instead. But told to drive ahead, that was what she had done, straight up into the rugged and lonely heart of the island.

It was somewhere up here that Moira Frensham, lost in drifting cloud, had driven off the road into one of the deep ravines beside it.

Moira, Justin, Roberta . . .

Now there was only Matthew left, if it was true that this boy had not shot him.

But why should she think for a moment that it was true? Her nerves began to get out of control again. She again heard herself shrieking hoarsely, "If you didn't kill them, who did? If you didn't do it, you saw it. You know all about it."

Quietly and obscenely he swore at her. There was not much sound of venom in it. It sounded more like something that he did automatically when he was startled. When the spasm was over, he added, "She was dead when I got there. Now keep your mind on your driving and let me think. This is a hell of a road. Why did you bring us this way?"

"Don't you like heights?" she asked.

"Never mind what I like." He plucked at his little rosebud mouth. "I tell you I'm trying to think, if only you'd give me a chance. Who got the stuff, that's what I need to know? Or is it still in that house somewhere?"

"Well, I can't tell you anything, so what do you want from me?" she asked. "Why do you want to come up here?"

"I didn't want to come up here. It was you picked this road. I just said, 'It's a hell of a road,' didn't I? I never wanted to come up here."

"You told me to drive ahead, so I drove ahead," she said.

"That's right, you did." He sounded as if he did not want to seem unreasonable. "Well, you can just go on till I tell you to stop. And keep quiet."

But Camilla felt a compulsion to go on talking. Silence gave her time to think of Roberta.

"Where did you spend last night?" she asked. "The police were out looking for you."

"I spent it in among a lot of bananas. Ate some of them too when I got hungry. They weren't ripe. Half-green. Gave me pains all night."

"Aren't you hungry now?"

"Of course I'm hungry."

"Then why don't you just give yourself up to the police? They're bound to catch you soon. You can't get off an island like this."

"There are a lot more ways of getting off an island than you know anything about," he answered. "Boats go out all the time. The little boats. All you need is money. Chris has got all that fixed up. He's good at fixing things, old Chris is. But I'm not going without those bloody diamonds and the police aren't going to get me till I've found out where they are. My bet is, Davy's got them,

154

though I'd have sworn that kid Julie didn't know enough about what was going on to tell him anything about them. Shows how wrong you can be . . . Look out!"

Camilla had just gone too near to the edge of the road for Bernie's liking. He had gone white at the glimpse that he had had of the depths below the sheer cliffs, a remote valley and a village, in which each little cottage had a still smaller, thatched hut in the garden, huts in which the cattle of the island were kept, since the hillsides were too steep for grazing. There was a small white church in the village, with a square tower with a little candle-snuffer steeple on top, like a miniature version of the cathedral in Funchal.

As she steered the car back to the centre of the road, Camilla said, "So Julie *was* in with you."

But did that have to mean, she wondered, that Alec Davy's reason for coming to Madeira had had nothing to do with getting an apology out of Roberta, but had been simply to get the diamonds from Joanne? Camilla's sense of trust in him was something that she had just been beginning to enjoy. It was beginning to seem something that might be important to her.

"Well," Bernie said thoughtfully, "what we thought was, she didn't really know what she'd got into. All she was supposed to know was she'd got to hold the job down here for a few weeks, and she got a kick out of feeling she was in on something big. She'd had a bad break in some other job she'd had, been accused of something she hadn't done or something, and wanted to get even. Fool of a reason for doing anything, but she was a bit of a fool all round, that's what I thought. Which shows, as I said, how wrong you can be. The little bitch must have got the whole plan out of Chris when he brought her in on the show without his even knowing what he was giving away. Yes, it just shows how you keep on learning all the time. She must have got it out of old Chris, told Davy . . ." His voice died away. Plucking at his small pink mouth again, he retired once more into deep thought.

There was fog ahead on the road now. The air suddenly felt damp and chill. Behind them the white Volkswagen was still the same distance away. There were two men in it. They looked relaxed enough to be tourists. On the other hand, they did not talk much to one another, did not slow down when the view became particularly spectacular, did not point out the beauties of the route to one another. Not only the driver but his passenger too kept his eyes on the road before them. Camilla felt that if her sight had been sharper, she would have found herself meeting their steady gaze in the driving-mirror.

"It's bloody cold up here," Bernie remarked after a few minutes. They had emerged from the patch of cloud, but the high mountain air was sharp. "I could do with a sweater. When do we get off this damned road?"

"We don't," Camilla said.

"How do you mean, we don't? When's the next turning off it?"

"There isn't one."

"Look, I'm not fooling," he said. "There'd better be a turning off it."

"I'm not fooling either," she said. "There isn't one."

"Where does it go then?"

"Nowhere."

His voice grew rougher. "What d'you mean, nowhere? Roads don't just go nowhere."

"This one does. It just goes up the mountain and stops."

"What did they make it for then?"

"Mostly for innocent tourists in buses, who want to take a look at the view."

"And you knew that all the time we've been coming up?"

"Oh yes. It's a famous view, a very beautiful one. You'll be glad to have seen it."

He told her what she could do with the view. Then for the first time since they had started out, turned in his seat and took a long look at the car behind them.

When he turned back to look at Camilla, his face had altered. It was as if its texture had changed. Its youthful softness had gone. The skin looked almost like bone, it was so taut and pallid. His knuckles became all projecting bone too as the fingers that had been loosely curved round the butt of the gun on his lap tightened.

"You did it on purpose," he said more quietly than he had spoken yet. "You knew what you were doing, driving me into a trap."

"I didn't think about it," she said truthfully. "I only did what you told me to."

"No turnings, a dead end and the police on our tail," he said. "You did it on purpose."

"You don't know that they're police," she said, "but if they are, let me warn you, they're probably armed. This isn't England."

"All right. Stop. Get out."

"What?" she said stupidly.

"Stop!" he shouted at her. "Get out!" He leant across her to tug at the handle of the door beside her and pushed it open. "Out fast!" He gave her a violent shove as he said it and as she tumbled out of the car into a bank of hydrangeas, he grabbed at the steering-wheel, slithered into the driving seat, slammed the door and drove on into another patch of fog ahead.

Bruised and dizzy, with the tall pine trees round her reeling crazily and with a sharp pain in her shoulder which had been wrenched as she fell, Camilla stayed where she was, trying to get her breath back. The other car, she thought, would stop. The men would get out and help her.

But the car did not stop. It went on at the same steady pace up the mountain road and disappeared after Bernie into the fog.

They were police, then. And it was Bernie that they wanted. And he was trapped all right.

The road ended at a point where tourists could get out of their buses and climb up wooden steps to a still greater height, to look across the deep valley to the jagged peaks on the far side of it. Not that Bernie would see much of valley or peaks to-day. Apart from his having too much else on his mind, there was too much cloud. The valley would be a gently steaming cauldron, and the peaks, if they showed above the fog, would seem to ride there in the air without support. Bernie would have room to turn his car and start down the hill again, but the police car could easily block off the entrance to the road.

Camilla picked herself up and rubbed her shoulder, which was hurting. She supposed that she was lucky. She could easily have been injured a good deal more seriously, might have broken something, or even, on a different stretch of road, gone over the edge. She could also have been in the car still when Bernie, if he did, tried to shoot it out with the police.

Meanwhile, in her cotton dress, without even a jacket, she was very cold. She had better start walking. Probably she would not have to walk far. There would be other cars along soon, or perhaps a bus. She picked her way out from among the hydrangeas and started down the road.

The air was fragrant with the strong scent of the pines and from somewhere came the sound of running water. The fog was not dense, but it stroked her skin with clammy fingers. She walked fast, and while she walked, it seemed to her, Roberta came to walk beside her.

Not the Roberta of the last few years, hobbling cautiously on crutches, but a vigorous and lovely young woman, full of self-confidence and gaiety. And no fool. That was a thing that Camilla had sometimes forgotten. Because Roberta had always been expert at making facts mean what she wanted them to, it didn't mean that she didn't see the facts for what they were. She had been self-centred and often unscrupulous, but she had never been stupid. She had been proved right about other people again and again. Hadn't she been right about both Julie Davy and Christopher? And she had been right about Camilla too, pointing out all the mistakes that she was making in her life with deadly shrewdness.

But that in itself had been a mistake, for Camilla had only resented it. Roberta's criticisms had never done her any good. The more successfully they had struck home, and the more they had hurt, the more they had merely angered Camilla. The things that Roberta had said about Christopher, for instance, had all been true and all unforgiveable. Poor Roberta, why had she made it so hard for people to love her?

Tears began to trickle out of Camilla's eyes as she walked. They were for Roberta and for Christopher, and of course for herself. Probably most of all for herself, which was a rather disgusting thought. She took off her glasses for a moment and did her best to wipe the tears away with the back of her hand. In the blurry scene around her the young Roberta faded from her side and instead Camilla suddenly saw sharply and clearly a vision of Roberta dead, with the blood on her chest.

Could she have killed herself? In her state of mind suicide wasn't impossible. But would a person shoot herself in the heart? Wouldn't she have put the gun to her temple? Perhaps not Roberta, who might have wanted to preserve her face, her last beauty. But Camilla had felt no impulse to believe what Bernie Pope had said about finding Roberta dead, with the gun beside her. Obviously, Camilla thought, Bernie had killed both Roberta and his father to get the diamonds for himself. There was really no mystery about the two murders. The only mystery was, where had the diamonds got to? Who had them?

Could it be Alec Davy after all? If it was true that Julie was a far cleverer girl than any of them had realised, he could have known of them. He had been in Funchal already when they had vanished. And he had had the same motive for taking them as any man. And all that talk about not knowing what he would do with a lot of money, if he had it . . .

Higher up the hill behind her, Camilla heard a car. It was coming down slowly through the mists. For a moment she was strongly inclined to leap into the bushes at the roadside and cower there out of sight till it was gone, in case the driver should turn out to be Bernie. But there was not really much chance that those two policemen would allow him to trick them into letting him escape from the trap into which she had led him. Only suppose they did it on purpose. Suppose they were less interested at the moment in catching him than in finding where he would go next.

She stood hesitating, intensely drawn by the shelter of the bushes. Then, as the car came closer, she decided that it did not sound like Roberta's. Staying where she was, she saw a grey Citroën come into view, with an elderly couple inside it.

The car stopped when the man, who was driving it, saw her signalling thumb.

He leant out and said carefully, "*Nao falo Portugues.*"

That she could not speak Portuguese happened to be one of Camilla's few phrases in the language also.

"English?" she asked hopefully.

He beamed at her. "That's right. You want a lift? Hop in." He reached over the back of his seat to the handle of the door behind him. "Come a long walk, haven't you?"

"You look frozen," his wife said. "There's a rug there. I'd wrap it round you till we get farther down."

They were both about sixty, a comfortable-looking couple with the odd likeness to one another that the long-married often acquire. Each voice was like an echo of the other, their hair had become the same shade of grey, and their two faces, one of which had certainly started out short and broad while the other had been long and narrow, had both acquired a similar, pink, indeterminate roundness.

"A very disappointing day," the man went on as he drove cautiously on down the winding road. "We were warned there was too much low cloud and we shouldn't see anything. But we're only spending a week here, so we didn't want to waste any time. We hired the car and it's really been very satisfactory. I've never driven over such roads, but we've really managed to see a great deal. Only not to-day. We've seen nothing but fog."

"And too cold for a nice picnic," his wife said. "We actually ate our lunch in the car. Very disappointing."

"Luckily we've learnt from experience how cold it can be high up," said the man. "We both brought warm jackets."

"Someone should have warned you," said the woman, "though of course it's all right if the sun is shining."

"Such a pity about to-day," said the man. "It's one of the great views of the island up there, I believe, and we saw nothing."

"Very disappointing," said his wife.

"Very disappointing," he echoed.

"We've been told it's quite spectacular."

"Yes, really spectacular. But not to-day."

"No. Such a pity. So disappointing."

There was a short silence, then the woman said, "Are your ears popping? Mine are."

But she did not really expect an answer. Neither of them seemed to expect more than an occasional yes and no from Camilla as they chatted placidly on about their holiday, their hotel, their excursions and the island. They did not ask what she had been doing up there, miles from any habitation, but seemed quite simply to assume that she had been taking a long walk by herself.

When they emerged from the region of cloud and the air grew warmer, the woman said with satisfaction that that was better and took off the knitted jacket that she had been wearing. The man stopped the car and took off his sweater. In the short pause Camilla listened for the sound of a car behind them, but there was nothing.

As they went on, the man asked, "Where d'you want to be dropped?"

"Oh, anywhere," Camilla said. "Anywhere in Funchal."

"We can just as easily take you to your door," he said. "We aren't in any hurry."

"No, really—just wherever you're going yourselves. I don't want to take you out of your way and I can get a taxi home."

Really she was wondering what she would find at home, the police again, their cars filling the road and taking some explaining even to this oblivious couple, or simply the closed door, still keeping the unspeakable secret of what was inside.

If that was it, if Roberta's body had not yet been found, she would never be able to face going in there alone again. She would go to Matthew instead.

"No, no, quite pointless," the man said. "We'll take you wherever you say. It's all the same to us which way we go. We're just cruising around." And with stubborn good nature he insisted on being told where to take her.

Camilla argued, but he was not to be cheated of his kindly act and in the end, as they drove down into the suburbs of Funchal, she deliberately misdirected him to a road at right angles to the road in which the Ellisons' house stood. Then she simply pointed at a house, said that that was it, thanked them with great warmth for the lift, and when they stopped, got out and stood at the gate, waving to them until they were out of sight.

As soon as they were, she started to run. But her knees were so shaky that she felt as if they might fold under her, her wrenched shoulder was aching and the sunlight blinded her. Standing still for a moment, she rubbed her shoulder, blinked, then began to walk towards the corner of the street.

As soon as she reached it and could see down the hill, she knew that Roberta had been found. There were three cars in the road outside her house, and several policemen. A small crowd of people had gathered on the opposite side of the road, which was as near as the police would let them come, and were watching with solemn, hungry interest. At first, as Camilla approached, one of the policemen shouted at her, gesturing to her to keep out of the way, but another recognised her and beckoned to her to come in. The heads in the crowd turned curiously to watch her as she went by. Her knees still felt weak and she grabbed at the doorpost for a moment before she could make herself enter the house.

Matthew came to meet her. He held out his arms to her and pulled her to him in a hard, brief embrace.

"Good God, where have you been?" he demanded. "You came here, didn't you? You found her. We saw your handbag. Why did you run away? Why didn't you come for me? I've been going mad with worry."

Before she could answer, Chefe Raposo appeared from behind Matthew.

"Is it true that you have been here?" he asked. "Do you know what has happened to your sister?"

All at once she was unable to speak. She only nodded and put out a hand to hold on to Matthew. He reached for a chair and thrust it under her.

"Then why did you go away without telling anyone?" the Chefe asked.

"I didn't—I was taken away—Bernie Pope was here —he made me drive away . . . Please, I think I'm going to be sick." She stumbled up from the chair and made a dash for the bathroom.

She was not sick, she only retched helplessly and painfully, then, as the spasms passed, stood leaning against the wall, feeling clammy all over.

That man was going to question her now and she was going to have to decide how much she was going to tell him of the things that Christopher had told her. She should have thought of that sooner. She had had all the afternoon, driving up the mountain and then down again, to think about it. But it had not seemed at the time a particularly urgent problem. It was not easy to think clearly about anything when you were in a car with Bernie, and on the way down the steady chat of those kind, dull people had afflicted her with a complete blankness of mind. But now she must take a decision.

Yet she had not arrived at one when she emerged from the bathroom. She had washed her face in cold water, combed her hair and swallowed two aspirins, but she had not decided on anything.

Matthew led her into the dining-room, thrust her into a chair and gave her some whisky. Both he and the Chefe watched her as she drank it. If the Chefe had questions to ask her, he appeared to be in no hurry. His expression was compassionate. After a moment, at a call from one of his men, he went out, saying that he would return immediately. Matthew topped up her glass a little, and poured out a drink for himself.

"Go on—say it," he said. "Why did I leave?"

"Why did you?" she asked. "You said you'd stay till I got back."

"She sent me away," he answered.

"Roberta sent you?"

"Yes."

"Why?"

"We quarrelled. She told me to get out. I oughtn't to have gone, of course. I oughtn't to have taken any notice. But the things she said got under my skin. . . . Oh hell, why talk about that now? I oughtn't to have gone, that's all. But she told me to get out. After all these years—can you believe it?—she told me to get out and not come back."

"What did you quarrel about?" Camilla asked, bewildered.

"Those ear-rings." His voice rose in a sudden shout that made her tired body jerk and quiver. "Those damned, bloody ear-rings!"

CHAPTER X

"I DON'T understand," said Camilla.

"I don't wonder." He apologised for shouting and began to walk up and down the room. The movement made the whisky swill around in his glass. Some of it spilled down his wrist and sleeve. "I swore to myself I wouldn't quarrel with her, Camilla. I did. I kept telling myself not to pay any attention to her. I understood the state she'd been in since Justin's death. I was sorry for her. But she went on and on about the ear-rings, saying they'd really vanished and how someone had taken them, but got scared at having so many police around and slipped them back into the box. Then she asked me, quite seriously, apparently, if I thought it could have been you."

"*Me*?"

"Yes, you." His voice reached a shout again. "You!"

"But why——?"

"Because——" It began in the same bellowing tone, then he deliberately checked himself and spoke very quietly. "Because you wanted to get rid of Joanne and stay on here, but you didn't want Roberta to realise it. And d'you know why you didn't? I'll give you three guesses. It's got its funny side——"

"Matthew, please."

"I'm sorry, I'm sorry. I've got such a sense of guilt . . ." He raked his fingers through his rough, grey hair. "What was I saying? Oh yes, the reason you'd taken the ear-rings. The very one you told me Julie suggested. You'd been reflecting on the fact that Roberta's rich and that you're her nearest relative and that probably she hadn't long to live. Well then, I lost my temper and told her I knew it was she who'd taken the ear-rings, meaning to plant them in Joanne's room, to get rid of her as she had Julie and so persuade you to stay on. I told her it was she who'd got

165

scared at having the police around and put the ear-rings back in the box. I told her too it was time she stopped behaving like a child and realised that other people had their lives to live. . . . D'you know, I believe it's the only time in my life I've ever kicked back at Roberta. I'm not sure it isn't the only time anyone ever has. Justin never did. He had a knack of going his own way, when he wanted to, without letting her realise that he wasn't going hers. Of course, it was the right way to handle her, but I'm not subtle enough for it. I've always taken the line of least resistance with her, telling myself I was being tactful and considerate. And just this once I didn't. Just this once I said what I thought. And she told me to get out of the house and not come back. Very harshly, very decisively. Get out and don't come back. After all these years. The very first time I said what I thought. . . ."

"But you did come back," Camilla said. "You came back and found her."

"Yes, I—I wanted to say I was sorry. I thought perhaps she'd be feeling sorry too by then." He pulled out a chair from the table and sat down. He sighed heavily. "Now I'll never know if she was. Not that it matters. A silly thing to worry about. The thing to remember is the old, good years. They were very good, you know. The four of us had something. But when Moira died it began to change. I somehow slipped into being dependant on Justin and Roberta. . . . . Well, why talk about that now?"

Why indeed? Camilla thought, and tried to fix her mind on what he had told her of Roberta's accusation that she had taken the ear-rings. Then the thought suddenly slipped into her mind, like a slimy little snake, that she was rich now. Moderately rich, at least. It gave her a sharp little thrill, followed by a wave of self-disgust. Were there any people, she wondered, who could honestly say that they ever kept their minds completely off money for more than a very short time?

"Matthew, if Roberta put the ear-rings in Joanne's

room," she said, "is there any possibility at all that she found out about the trick suitcase? Could she have found the diamonds?"

"Diamonds?" he said sharply.

"Oh, of course, you don't know . . ."

"But you do, apparently. What do you know? And how did you get to know it?"

She felt the nausea again that came with indecision. She shut her eyes to blot out Matthew's hard, inquiring stare. Some day, she supposed, she would look back to this time and see how she ought to have acted. Christopher would mean less to her. Loyalty to him, or what had been her image of him, would seem an immature and regrettably muddled emotion.

"Bernie told me," she answered.

"Told you there were diamonds in that suitcase?"

"Yes."

"And you think Roberta found them?"

"No, I don't. Oh, I don't know. I asked you, is it possible?"

"That she found some stolen diamonds and kept them? Roberta?" He looked for a moment as if he were going to deny it explosively, then his face grew thoughtful. He moved away from Camilla. Absently he reached for the whisky bottle, but before he had refilled his glass, seemed suddenly to become aware of what he was doing, irritably put the bottle down and started to walk up and down the room again.

"That she found them is possible," he said, "just as you say, when she was looking for a place to plant the ear-rings on Joanne. But that she'd keep them . . . Do *you* think that's possible?"

"I don't think so, but—well—if she didn't, who did?"

"The normal Roberta couldn't have done it," he said. "But as she's been these last few weeks, it isn't, it doesn't strike me, as absolutely impossible. But just suppose she took them, where did she hide them? The police have been through this house twice, the second time very thoroughly.

And she couldn't get out of it alone. So where are they now?"

"I don't know. I haven't any idea. I'd say Bernie must have got hold of them somehow, except that he seemed crazy to find out from me where they were. That's why he took me with him. I don't think——"

But at that moment she began to think.

She thought of the sitting-room as it had been when she walked in and found Roberta dead there. The picture of it, which had been with her ever since that moment, came back to her suddenly, with complete clarity and she saw now what had been missing, what it was the absence of which had gone on haunting her all the time, although she had not known what it was. Something she was so used to seeing. The rubber tips of Roberta's crutches. The light metal crutches themselves had been there, lying where they had dropped when she fell, but the tips had been missing.

"Her crutches!" she said in an astonished voice. "They're hollow——"

That was as far as she got, for Matthew's face brightened in a most curious way, as if the new idea, for the moment, meant more to him than grief. He wheeled to the door.

"Senhor Chefe!" he called out. "Senhor Chefe, what have you done with Mrs. Ellison's crutches?"

The Chefe emerged from the sitting-room, where Roberta's body, after it had been examined by the police surgeon, photographed, and discussed by a group of busy, tired men, had just been lifted on to a stretcher to be carried out to a waiting ambulance. The ambulance was a discreet dark blue, unlike the hearses of Madeira, which are gaily decorated in glittering gold on black and give that last progress an air of royal festivity.

"So you have thought of that too." The Chefe had the two light metal crutches in his hand. "But so has someone else. If your suspicions are correct, we are too late." He came into the dining-room and laid the crutches down on the table. "Empty," he said.

"Yes, I see," said Matthew.

"But what did you hope to find there, Mr. Frensham? Are you merely guessing, or have you found out anything that could help us? Has Miss Carey perhaps been able to tell you something?"

"Just an idea we had," said Matthew. "Shall I tell him about it, Camilla, or will you?"

She remained silent and Matthew began to talk. He sounded embarrassed, as if he were wishing now that he had never said anything about the crutches, because it meant telling the Chefe of their suspicions of Roberta, but he told the story in a far more orderly fashion than Camilla would have found possible herself. He began with the story of Julie Davy, her arrival, Roberta's apparent liking for her, Camilla's intention of returning home, then the discovery in Julie's drawer of the cosmetics from Godhino's, of Julie's immediate insistence on leaving and Roberta's later admission that she herself had put the things in Julie's drawer to get rid of her.

The Chefe had sat down and was leaning back in his chair, listening intently. There was an air of slight puzzlement in his earnest attention, as if it were not clear to him why the story had to begin so far back, or else, perhaps, why he had not been told all this before. But he did not interrupt with questions, and sat quite still, as if, among other things, he were giving himself a little rest while he had the chance.

Matthew went on, "Then Miss Willis came out to take Miss Davy's place. Neither Miss Carey nor I liked Miss Willis, but Mrs. Ellison seemed to take a great fancy to her. She wouldn't have anything said against her. I was uneasy, but Mrs. Ellison—well, her mind seemed to be made up,. and she wasn't an easy woman to argue with. But then one day she announced to Miss Carey that a pair of her ear-rings had disappeared, and she believed—she seemed to believe—that Miss Willis had stolen them."

Without moving his head, the Chefe turned his dark eyes

on Camilla. She nodded her confirmation of what Matthew had said.

"But this time, naturally," he continued, "we didn't believe Mrs. Ellison. We thought that she was trying to repeat what she'd done before in a slightly different form. I think we both warned her that it was dangerous. But this time we couldn't budge her. We never managed to make her withdraw the accusation. But yesterday evening, after you'd all gone, she insisted on opening her jewel-case to show us that the ear-rings weren't there—and there they were. Well, of course, any of us could have put them back, including Mrs. Ellison herself, as well as Miss Willis, so finding them didn't mean much. But on the whole I'm still inclined to believe that our first guess was right. Mrs. Ellison put those ear-rings in Miss Willis's room, meaning to have them discovered there and then to sack the girl. And if Mrs. Ellison really did do that, you see, she might have thought of that suitcase as a good place for hiding the ear-rings and so stumbled on the trick of it and found what was hidden inside it."

"And that was?" the Chefe asked.

"Diamonds," Camilla said. "Stolen from the Countess of Engleton. Seventy-five thousands pounds' worth. Bernie Pope told me."

It did not worry her that this was not true. Step by step, she had committed herself to protecting Christopher. Not that that would go on if he appeared to have had anything to do with Roberta's death. But she was too sure of Bernie's guilt to worry over Christopher's share in it.

"So your theory," the Chefe said, picking his words slowly as if the effort of speaking English were increasing with his tiredness, "is that Mrs. Ellison found these diamonds some days ago and concealed them in these hollow crutches, but still proceeded with her accusation that Miss Willis had stolen her ear-rings, knowing that Miss Willis would not dare to protest."

"And not knowing, you see," Matthew said, "that the Popes were coming, and that they would expect the diamonds to be handed over to them, and that when Miss Willis couldn't do that, they would come here, looking for them."

"And Mrs. Ellison shot Louis Pope?"

Matthew shook his head. "I told you before, I don't think she had a gun. I don't think she could shoot. I think Bernie shot him, meaning to get away with all the loot himself. But something frightened him off before he had time to start searching—perhaps the arrival of Mr. Peters —and he ran away. But to-day he came back and hunted again, and this time Mrs. Ellison interfered and so he shot her."

"And when he saw the crutches lying there," the Chefe said, "it occurred to this Bernie that crutches are hollow, so he looked inside them and found the diamonds."

"Well?"

"It is a nice theory." The Chefe's tone was dampening. "A nice theory, yes. There is only one thing wrong with it, and that is that it is not correct."

He pulled himself slowly to his feet, looking reluctant to leave the chair in which he had briefly rested.

"It happens that this house was being watched," he said. "There were two of my men all day in the garden opposite. They saw Bernie Pope arrive at the house, try the front door, then go round to the back. They were about to follow, since their orders were to arrest him, when Miss Carey drove up and went quickly into the house. Almost immediately she and Pope came out together, got into the car and drove away. She was obviously being compelled to do this, so for her safety, my men did not interfere, but followed at a distance. So you see, young Mr. Pope had very little time in this house. He had time, perhaps, to commit the murder, if he did it instantly on entering, but not to have clever ideas and look inside and empty hollow crutches."

"I see," Matthew said thoughtfully. "But if your men were watching the house . . ."

"Yes?"

171

"Didn't they see anyone besides Pope and Miss Carey come and go?"

"They did indeed, Mr. Frensham. They saw you."

"Yes, of course. But no one else?"

"No one else."

"That," Matthew said, "is a very unpleasant discovery."

The Chefe smiled slightly. "It just happens, however, that Mrs. Ellison was seen alive after you left the house. If you remember, she came to the door with you. You appeared to be quarrelling, or at least arguing, and she stood in the doorway for a moment, looking after you as you walked away. It is an unfortunate fact, besides, that there was no watch being kept on the back of the house. The murderer almost certainly approached it through the banana plantation and climbed the wall into the garden."

"That would have been taking a pretty big risk, wouldn't it?" Matthew said. "He could have been seen by anyone in the next-door houses."

"Yes, and naturally we have inquired already if anyone was seen. But on one side, as you know, live an elderly couple who are accustomed to sleep in the afternoon, and on the other side is a family with young children, all of whom had gone down to the sea for the day. So the murderer was lucky. Or let us say, he took the lesser risk, coming in through the garden, rather than walking boldly up to the front door." He turned to Camilla. "Miss Carey, you have not told us yet how you escaped from the car and succeeded in returning home."

"He threw me out," she said. "He knew we were being followed and when he discovered we were driving into a dead end, he threw me out. I don't know why—to have more freedom of action, perhaps. He had a gun."

"He had?" the Chefe said.

"Yes, he said he found it here beside my sister, and only picked it up when he heard me come in."

"So it could have been suicide," said Matthew.

"Yes—yes, there is that possibility. Her state of mind ———"

The telephone rang.

"A moment, please," the Chefe said and left them.

They could hear him, from the dining-room, talking into the telephone. Camilla saw that Matthew was listening intently. After a moment he translated. "Bernie. I think they've got him. But there's something also about Peters. About his going swimming." He dropped into the chair in which the Chefe had been sitting. "You know that was a very nasty moment for me just now, when our Chefe —do you know, by the way, that Raposo means fox?—yes, a very nasty moment when the foxy fellow said that apart from you and Bernie, I was the only person who'd been seen coming in and out of the house. What did you think when you heard it?"

"I didn't think," Camilla said. "I can't think."

Out in the hall she heard the words, "Senhor Peters," repeated, and they sent a sharp little shiver up her spine.

"Perhaps if I could think of a reason why you should steal Roberta's ear-rings and go poking around in Joanne's room and find the diamonds, I might think you'd killed her," she went on. "But Roberta didn't take them, you know. We've been talking like idiots. She didn't commit suicide either. I want some more whisky." She held out her glass.

"Watch it," Matthew said. "You're in a state when you could get drunk on emotion by itself." But he got up and refilled her glass for her.

"I'd like to get drunk," she said. "At the moment it seems the only thing to do."

She took a long swallow.

"Roberta told me I drank too much," she said. "She was always telling me things about myself. They were generally right, which made it worse. She was right about other people too. Julie. Christopher. And she told me . . ."

Matthew had been watching her steadily. As she stopped abruptly, he asked, "What is it, Camilla?"

She looked down quickly, but not before their eyes had met. She hesitated, then said, "Nothing."

"That's a lie," he said.

"Yes, it's a lie," she agreed.

"You saw—it could have been a ghost."

"I heard one. I heard one tell me who stole the ear-rings and why—and so, I suppose, who found the diamonds, and shot Louis Pope."

"And killed Roberta?"

"Yes."

"Who?"

"It was you, wasn't it, Matthew?"

For an instant, his expression changed terrifyingly. She had never seen such violence in a pair of human eyes before. But the house was full of policemen. He passed a hand over his face, presenting her with what she thought of as his policeman's face, neutral and attentive.

"Explain yourself, my dear," he said, quite gently.

"Roberta told me," Camilla said. "She said—she said you were fond of me . . ."

"And she was right. But is that wicked? Does it make me a thief and a murderer?"

"But you wanted me to stay on here, didn't you?"

"Of course I did. I told you so myself, didn't I? For Roberta's sake."

"Only for Roberta's?"

"Well, perhaps not . . ."

"And Roberta herself put it into your head how to do it by what she did to Julie. You simply copied her. You took her ear-rings, knowing she'd miss them at once, and you were going to put them in Joanne's room, in her suitcase, for Roberta to find, so that she'd sack Joanne. You weren't thinking of either theft or murder then. It was just a very little misdemeanour you were committing. But when you handled that suitcase, you discovered the false bottom. You'd know about things like that, I suppose. You'd spot it easily. And inside were the diamonds. . . . I don't think you thought any more about Roberta or me after that, Matthew. It's odd, I never thought of you as

174

caring much about money, but I suppose you must have wanted it terribly this past year or two."

He smiled. "Go on."

"Oh, I know I couldn't prove any of it. But who but you would have known that it was safe to come back here this afternoon through the garden—that the old couple would be asleep and the other people at the sea? And whom else would Roberta have protected?"

"Protected? Roberta?"

"Yes, when she heard the shot that killed Louis Pope and knew you were in the house. She'd asked you to come over, hadn't she? She was expecting you. And she'd either seen you come in from her bedroom window, or heard you speak, or recognised your step. Then she heard the shot and she was scared to go out. But the first thing she asked me when I went in and found her sitting there in a state of shock, trying to make up her mind what to do, was whether it was you who'd been killed. And when she knew it wasn't, she decided to say nothing."

"But where was her problem?" Matthew asked. "If any of this were true, why shouldn't she simply have turned me in?"

"You were her very dear friend," Camilla said. "The only one left. And I think she thought you'd simply shot an intruder to protect her. I suppose the gun was Pope's and you got it away from him. And I think it was only to-day, when Roberta heard about the trick suitcase, that she began to wonder about what you'd really done yesterday. And when I left the two of you alone together this morning, she asked you some questions and you quarrelled and you gave yourself away to her, and so you came back over the garden wall and killed her. And taking the rubber tips off her crutches was a delicate touch you added to make it look as if she could have had the diamonds there and someone else—it might have been Bernie—had killed her and taken them. It was just your bad luck that I came into the house so soon after Bernie that he couldn't have had time to do that. But you saw us come out of the house and drive up the hill, didn't you, and you didn't know what we were going to do, so you thought it safest to come back here and find Roberta and give the alarm yourself."

"And what are you going to do about all this now?" Matthew was kneading his big hands together. It looked as if he were trying to crush something between them. At the same time he was giving a strange, distorted smile. "I've made up cases like this against people myself—felt so very sure of them—and in the end, there's so little you can do."

"But they'll find the diamonds, won't they, once they think of it?" Camilla watched his hands with an uneasy sort of fascination, then raised her eyes reluctantly again to meet the hard eyes in his taut, battered-looking face. Almost inaudibly she added, "I'm never much good at knowing what to do. Couldn't you do something about it?"

For an instant he looked startled, then his face changed, settling into lines of extreme sadness and exhaustion. "Ah. I see. Yes," he said, "there's that. You'll see they do look for the diamonds, of course. So perhaps it would be best . . . I don't know. I'll have to think. But keep out of my way!" he added in a thick voice. "Do you understand? When the police go, leave this house. Go to a hotel. I'm warning you. Don't let me see you again."

Outside in the hall some orders were being given. There was a good deal of movement among the men there. Then the door opened and the Chefe came in. He was looking a little more cheerful than usual. A light almost of self-satisfaction shone in his dark eyes.

"My men have arrested Bernard Pope," he announced. "It was a very clever thing that you did, Miss Carey, taking him up the road to Eira do Serado. There was no escape for him. When he saw it, he did not shoot, but went peaceably. He is now at the *Policia*. I am told he denies having any diamonds and having killed anybody, but

176

I shall go now to interrogate him. He is asking for Mr. Peters. I do not know why. But the curious thing is that Mr. Peters cannot be found. It is very curious. Since he went swimming this morning with you, Miss Carey, he has not been seen. Do you know anything of his whereabouts? Can you help us to find him?"

She only looked at him vacantly. Her mind had taken a plunge into an abyss and she could not drag herself out of it. After meeting her look, he did not press the question. He spoke to Matthew.

"My men have just removed the body of Mrs. Ellison. But I do not think Miss Carey should stay here alone. She has suffered a very severe shock. Has she a woman friend with whom she could stay, or who would come here to stay with her? She should call a doctor, take a sedative and rest."

Matthew did not answer or turn round, but went on staring out of the window.

Camilla got unsteadily to her feet. The whisky perhaps had not been a good idea, though it had loosened her tongue and temporarily blunted her capacity for feeling.

"I don't want a doctor," she said. "I'll go to a hotel. Please tell me what you mean about Mr. Peters disappearing."

"Simply that," the Chefe said. "He has disappeared. You and he went down to the bathing-place at Reid's together, then you were seen to go up in the lift by yourself. The boy who was working the lift remembered you. But he did not see Mr. Peters. And Mr. Peters did not have lunch in the hotel and the clothes that he took off to swim are where he threw them down on the bed in his room. It looks almost as if he swam out to sea and never came back. But why should he do that? Well, I must go. Can I drive you to a hotel, Miss Carey, or will Mr. Frensham do that?"

"I'd be very grateful if you would," Camilla replied. "Can you wait a minute or two while I pack a few things?"

"Of course."

Without looking at Matthew she left the room, went to her bedroom, packed the things that she needed for the night into a little overnight bag and told the Chefe that she was ready.

He took her by the arm, having noticed the unsteadiness of her walk, how she took uncertain side-steps and blundered into things, almost as if she could not see. As he guided her out to the car, she heard Matthew, behind her, say her name once, abruptly and loudly, as if he were protesting about something, then a second time in a tone of total emptiness.

She did not look round or answer. She got into the police car, sat back and shut her eyes. When the Chefe asked her which hotel she preferred, she said that she did not know, and when he suggested one, nodded. He took her to one of the new ones overlooking the harbour, spoke to the reception-clerk, arranged for her to have a room, and only left her when she had been handed over to a maid who took her to her room and presently, without Camilla having ordered it, brought her coffee and sand-wiches.

The room had a balcony and Camilla sat on it for a long time in the darkness, looking out over the Bay of Funchal, at the bright lights of a new cruise-ship in the harbour, at a garish electric sign that turned continuously, casting different coloured reflections on to the water, and at the darkness beyond, dotted with a few small moving lights of fishing boats putting out to sea.

Was Christopher perhaps in one of those small boats? Had Bernie been telling the truth when he said that Christopher had a way fixed up of leaving the island? Or had Christopher simply swum out to sea and not come back, because he had nothing left to come back for? When would she know what had happened to him?

At last she went to bed, but she did not sleep. She was filled with haunting, changing fears, the backwash of the responsibility that she had accepted that evening. Frightened of responsibility? That was what she had always thought she was. And she was indeed, after taking on herself a bigger one than she ever had in her life. That, at least, was how it appeared as she waited wearily for the long night hours to pass.

She had her breakfast sent to her room, and soon afterwards the Chefe came to see her. He told her to prepare herself for more bad news, yet he then told it badly, as if he had a suspicion that she might not be unprepared for it. An hour or two after the police had left her sister's house, he said, Matthew Frensham had been seen by a neighbour to take his car out of the garage. He had then driven up the road to Eira do Serado and over the edge at almost the very spot where his wife had been killed a few years before. Beside his typewriter at home, on top of the heap of unfinished manuscript of his life-story, he had left a handwritten message. It ran, "I stole the diamonds. I killed Louis Pope. I killed Roberta Ellison. I am about to kill myself. No one else is to blame."

Weighing the message down on the pile of typewritten sheets were three small wash-leather bags, full of diamonds.

CHAPTER XI

IT WAS ABOUT a month later that Camilla was rung up in her little Highgate flat by Helen Peters. Helen wanted Camilla to come to see her. She asked her to come to the office over the Knightsbridge restaurant, the smallest and the newest of the three that the Peterses owned, but already the most successful. On the telephone Helen said very little, only that she thought that it was time for her and Camilla to have a talk.

Camilla almost asked her if she had had any news of Christopher, but decided that the question could wait, and next day, at five o'clock presented herself at the door of the restaurant.

It did not open officially until six, but the door was unfastened. She opened it and went in. It was the restaurant in which she had painted the mural which had brought her and Christopher together again after their long separation. It had been an abstract, perhaps too delicate in design for the space that it occupied, but she had been pleased with it at the time. She half-dreaded seeing it now. So she was almost as relieved as she was angry to find that the wall where it had been was now covered in a wallpaper of green and red, that simulated damask. A very elaborate crystal lighting-fixture projected from the centre of it, and there had been other changes in the small room. There was a general atmosphere of gilt and red velvet, of candle-light and shadows. Quite well done, if you liked that kind of thing. And as unlike as possible to the cool-looking brightness of the room as it had been before.

That was what Helen had intended, of course, Camilla thought, as a man in a white jacket, who had been going round inspecting the tables and here and there rearranging the flowers on them, approached her and asked her what she wanted. When Helen spent what had certainly been a good deal of money on completely redecorating a room that should not have needed it for a few years, it must have been to blot out what it had been, to forget as much as she could as quickly as possible.

Camilla told the man that she had come to see Mrs. Peters and he took her upstairs to the room over the restaurant, where Helen, looking thinner than when Camilla had seen her last, more restless, more keyed-up, but as modish and self-assured as ever, got up quickly from behind a big, black-topped, Swedish desk and came to meet her.

Helen did not offer her hand, but smiled in a quite friendly way and did offer a drink. She was a tall woman, with hair that had turned prematurely to gleaming silver-grey and very large, dark eyes with heavy lids and thick lashes.

"I hope you don't mind too much about the mural," she

said as she sat down again at the desk with Camilla facing her in a curiously shaped but comfortable chair covered in yellow tweed. Both women had glasses of sherry. "You worked so hard on it. I didn't think of it when I asked you to come here."

On the contrary, Camilla thought, it had been one of the reasons why she had been asked to come. She was to be shown that all that hard work, and other things besides, had gone for nothing.

But could you blame Helen? Camilla met her rather wry smile with one of her own.

"It was yours, you paid for it, you could do what you liked with it."

"Oh yes, I know. But I'd understand if you were angry." Helen stroked the yellow tweed of the chair that she was sitting in with a long, pointed, red nail, which made a rasping sound like tearing cloth. She had not touched her drink. "I really wanted to see you again to ask if you'd had any news of Christopher."

"I was thinking of asking you that," Camilla said.

"Then you've heard nothing."

"No. And I don't think I really expect to."

"Because you believe he's dead."

"I'm not sure. Not necessarily."

Helen clicked her tongue in a way that expressed exasperation rather than anything else.

"Isn't it like him," she said, "to swim off into the blue without telling anyone he was going to do it? Why couldn't he leave a note behind, as that other man did? You've no idea of the legal complications it's let me in for. I don't know how long it's going to be before he can be 'presumed dead,' as they say. Meanwhile, of course, I can't get married."

"You want to get married, then?"

"Well, what do you think? Christopher and I only stuck together for the sake of the children and the business. Not that I was ever sure there was any point in it, from the point of view of the children. They didn't thrive on it.

They're the most neurotic brats you ever met. Didn't he tell you about Maurice?"

"No."

Helen gave her staccato little laugh. "Just like him again. Secretive. Left you to think you were leaving me desolate. Terribly unfair on you, really, just as the way he vanished from Madeira is abominably unfair on me. Of course, if that miserable Bernie hadn't come out with his story that Christopher had a way fixed up of getting away from the island, I don't suppose there'd have been any problems. It would have been accepted as an accidental drowning, swimming too far out, cramp, that sort of thing. And that's what I really believe. He was a most unsuicidal character. On the other hand, I wouldn't put it past him to have got to the Canaries somehow, or Tangier, or God knows where and have got in with the local crooks and be starting up a nice restaurant there already. Or gone as a mercenary in the Congo, or what-have-you. And he just might, when he's utterly and finally fed up with himself, go into a monastery and have a try at being saintly." She fixed her dark, shadowy eyes on Camilla's. "I wish you'd tell me what you really believe."

Camilla spoke without irony. "I think, you know, you know him far better than I do."

"Yes, I probably do. But you were there."

"Then I think . . ." Camilla played with the stem of the sherry glass on the table at her elbow. Neither of them seemed to want the drinks with which Helen had provided them. "I think he was tired of everything. His life. Me. You. Crime. Honesty. When he talked to me down on the rocks that day, I got the feeling he was telling me so much because he'd arrived at a dead end. The way that tricky plot with the diamonds had gone wrong gave him the taste of failure. Something he wasn't used to. There was always such an air of success about him. But whether that dead end meant suicide or a new start somewhere, I honestly don't know. . . . By the way, haven't you been troubled by the police?"

"Me?" Helen gave another abrupt laugh. "They've nothing on me. They'd nothing on Christopher. It isn't a crime to know a crook. If Louis liked to patronise one of our restaurants and have an occasional chat with the proprietor, could that be held against us? And in the early days, when Christopher really had far more to do with Louis than he did later, he was lucky enough to keep clear of the police. If that awful Bernie hadn't talked as much as he did, but kept his mouth shut, as Joanne had the sense to do, I don't think we'd have had a single detective round. As it was, they came, they asked me questions and went away again, seeing they couldn't get anywhere."

"I suppose Bernie will get a quite heavy sentence," Camilla said.

Helen shrugged her thin shoulders. "Probably."

"And Joanne?"

"Remains to be seen. She's clung to it that she knew nothing about the false bottom to the suitcase, and in any case, officially she's a first offender."

"And Julie Davy?"

"That child? What can they do to her? It isn't a crime to take a job as a lady's companion without meaning to stay in it for more than a few weeks. *Au pair* girls do it all the time."

"But is that really all she did?"

"Absolutely all. She didn't know a thing about why she was going to be paid to do just that."

"Are you sure? Are you sure she didn't know about the suitcase and what was going to be in it?"

"Look," Helen said impatiently, "do you think Louis was an amateur? He was a horrid little man, he'd got us where he wanted us and when we wanted to go straight—or I did, anyway, I'm not so sure that Christopher ever could have—Louis wouldn't let go. So that man in Madeira who finished him off would have been my friend for life, if he'd lived. But Louis wasn't an amateur and he wasn't a fool. He wouldn't have let a girl like that, whom he was just trying out, so to speak, know a single thing she didn't need to. No, if it matters to you, that girl was innocent as a babe unborn—well, almost—and it's lucky for her things went as they did, because the chances are she'll have been frightened off a life of crime." She gave Camilla another of her penetrating stares. "Why *does* it matter to you?"

Camilla drank a little of the sherry that she did not want. "I don't like loose ends," she said.

"My God, nor do I!" Helen said viciously. "And the way that bastard Christopher's left things . . . Well, perhaps after all he's dead and I'm being a bitch, holding it against him. If he's dead, good luck to him. He'll need it." She sipped her sherry too, then quickly drank off the rest. "I'm sorry about that mural, Cam, I really am. Perhaps if I'd waited till I'd seen you again, I shouldn't have felt I had to do anything about it."

"It's all right," Camilla said. "I'm rather glad it's gone really."

"We must meet again sometime. Perhaps you'd come here some evening and have dinner with Maurice and me."

"Thank you, that would be nice."

"I'll telephone."

"Yes, do."

The interview petered out to its end, both women knowing that with luck they need never see or think of one another again.

Helen went down the stairs with Camilla and saw her to the door, which a waiter was holding open for the first diners who were just getting out of their taxi.

There was a faint nip of autumn in the air. The leaves of the plane trees were turning rusty. Camilla walked slowly along Knightsbridge, loitering past Harrods, looking in all the windows. She had another appointment presently, but she had half an hour to fill in.

When she walked on, she soon stopped again at the window of an antique shop. It was purely for diversion. She had no thought of buying anything. She was still unused to the fact that she had become a modestly wealthy woman, and when she thought about it, was assailed by feelings of guilt. Why should the small, carefully garnered fortunes of all those dead aunts and uncles of Justin's, none of whom had ever set eyes on her, be handed on to her? The situation had induced a curious mood of irrational anxiety in her, which was making her work harder than ever and she was very thankful that a few days ago a publisher had just signed her up for a series of book-jackets. And she did not even think of taking a taxi to the Soho restaurant where she was to meet Alec Davy, but went by bus, then walked.

She had met Alec once before since they had both returned from Madeira and it had not been a great success. Camilla had felt totally unable to talk about what had happened in Funchal and yet had not been able to think of anything else. They had had an uneasy, silent lunch together and when they separated after it, Camilla had thought that that would be the last that she would ever see of him. But last night he had telephoned, saying that he was going to be in London for the day and had asked her to have dinner with him. She had almost refused, then had agreed, and immediately, until about half an hour ago, regretted it. But her talk with Helen had cleared certain cobwebs from her mind. When Alec, who was waiting for her in the cocktail lounge of the restaurant, lumbered to his feet to greet her, she was glad to see him.

"But you've changed," he exclaimed at once as she dropped into a chair at his side. "You look as if you've shed about five years—or anyway, some enormous burden. What's happened?"

"I've just been shedding burdens right and left," she said. "I'm beginning to realise it's a wonderful feeling."

"It must be," he said, and contemplated her thoughtfully. "You look—well, relaxed in a way I haven't seen you before. Am I going to be told anything about those burdens?"

"If you like—— It's only—oh, it's just been an enormous

load of suspicion that I've had on my mind. Suspicion of everyone. Ever since that day when Roberta told me about Julie ordering those things from Godhino's, I've felt quite ill from it. And now a lot of it only looks absurd. D'you know, I even played a little with the idea that it was Roberta who'd stolen those diamonds from Joanne? And when Christopher told me you'd obviously come to Funchal to look for them, because Julie must have known about them all along, I almost believed him. And I thought Christopher could have killed Pope——"

"Just a minute," Alec interrupted. "You thought I'd come to Funchal to get the diamonds?"

"Yes, I did. No, I didn't. Well, I played with the idea," she admitted. "But now I've just found out for certain that Julie didn't know about them, so she couldn't have told you, so I know that couldn't have been why you came, and so . . ." She began to laugh as at some abysmal absurdity.

He did not join in, but went on looking at her inquiringly. "And that was one of the burdens you've been carrying—that you've just shed? I mean, it mattered to you whether or not I'd told the truth about why I was in Funchal?"

She nodded. "Oh yes, it mattered."

His big, expressive ears turned pink with pleasure.

"And I almost didn't telephone," he said. "I suspected —I suspected quite feverishly—you wouldn't have any time for me at all. Now what shall we have to drink? Would champagne be nice for a change?"

>>> If you've enjoyed this book and would like to discover more great vintage crime and thriller titles, as well as the most exciting crime and thriller authors writing today, visit: >>>

The Murder Room
Where Criminal Minds Meet

themurderroom.com